-Missing from-
HAYMARKET SQUARE

HARRIETTE GILLEM ROBINET

ALADDIN PAPERBACKS
New York   London   Toronto   Sydney   Singapore

This book is a work of fiction. Any references to historical events, real people, or real locales are used fictitiously. Other names, characters, places, and incidents are the product of the author's imagination, and any resemblance to actual events or locales or persons, living or dead, is entirely coincidental.

First Aladdin Paperbacks edition January 2003

Text copyright © 2001 by Harriette Gillem Robinet
The song, "Eight-Hour Day Song," on pages 4 and 71, and flyer, on page 112, courtesy of William J. Adelman, Professor Emeritus, University of Illinois, Institute of Labor and Industrial Relations.

ALADDIN PAPERBACKS
An imprint of Simon & Schuster
Children's Publishing Division
1230 Avenue of the Americas
New York, NY 10020

Also available in an Atheneum Books for Young Readers hardcover edition. The text of this book was set in Janson Text.

Printed in the United States of America
2 4 6 8 10 9 7 5 3 1

The Library of Congress has cataloged the hardcover edition as follows:
Robinet, Harriette.
Missing from Haymarket square / Harriette Gillem Robinet,
p.cm.
Summary: Three children in Chicago in 1886 experience the Haymarket Riot in response to exploitative working conditions.
ISBN 0-689-83895-6 (hc.)
1. Haymarket Square Riot, Chicago, Ill., 18860—Juvenile fiction. [1. Haymarket Square Riot, Chicago, Ill., 1886—Fiction.]I. Title.
PZ7.R553 Cj 2001
[Fic]—dc21   99-088710

ISBN 0-689-85490-0 (Aladdin pbk.)

Books by Harriette Gillem Robinet

Ride the Red Cycle

Children of the Fire

Mississippi Chariot

If You Please, President Lincoln

Washington City Is Burning

The Twins, the Pirates, and the Battle of New Orleans

Forty Acres and Maybe a Mule

Walking to the Bus-Rider Blues

Missing from Haymarket Square

"Eight-Hour Day Song"

We mean to make things over,
We're tired of toil for naught,
But bare enough to live on
Never an hour for thought.
We want to feel the sunshine
We want to smell the flowers
We're sure that God has willed it,
And we mean to have eight hours.
We're summoning our forces,
From shipyard, shop, and mill:
Eight hours for work,
Eight hours for rest,
Eight hours for what we will.

CHAPTER ONE

That spring evening Dinah Bell walked carefully, trying not to stumble. Sunlight flickered on her brown face, and for a moment she closed her large black eyes. The family could starve, she thought; our little Josef has already died. We three children must do humbug, but I hate it.

The setting sun on Chicago's State Street lit windows so they shone like gold, windows in five-story buildings raised after Chicago's great fire in the fall of 1871.

It was now the spring of 1886, and the city was alive with new businesses and factories. However, there were no factories on State Street. Horse-drawn carriages passed, carrying wealthy families.

A rich lady in one of the carriages frowned at Dinah. Dinah steadied herself by holding the brass ring of a hitching post for horses. Why did the lady frown? Everyone whispered that Dinah was pretty. She touched her long black braid, which she had wrapped around her head like an olive wreath. She thought it made her look grand, like a girl in a Greek statue she once saw.

But she wore no bonnet, as someone noble would; a tattered shawl served as her head scarf. And worse still, she was dirty. She was not at all like the ladies in their long silk and satin dresses who strolled past her.

Taking a deep breath, she glanced over her shoulder. Several yards behind was blue-eyed Olive Schaffer, a recent immigrant who wore clothes as dirty and patched as Dinah's. Olive pulled a shawl to cover her grimy, butter white hair.

Like Dinah, she was twelve years old and ready for humbug. Olive was Dinah's good friend. Recent immigrants didn't seem to care that Dinah's people were of African ancestry and had been slaves only twenty years before.

Dinah glanced onto the street. At the curb their dog, Napoleon, trotted almost invisible in shadows. Good dog, he was ready. A brindled black on brown color, Napoleon's short-legged body was round like a sausage. At the thought, Dinah licked her lips. Humbug meant food. That was the only reason they did it.

On the other side of State Street sixteen-year-old, blue-eyed Ben Schaffer—Olive's brother—strolled, whistling, one hand in a pocket. He looked relaxed, but Dinah knew that he was testing the rock in his pocket and watching for danger.

Dinah knew that Ben hated humbug as much as she did. However, it was his little brother who had died, and he knew how important humbug was. His straw-colored hair stuck out from under a workman's cap, and his soiled workman's overalls seemed out of place among the gentlemen in suits and top hats who paraded on State Street.

Dinah searched the block around them. No police in sight. Pampered pooches of the rich met and sniffed one another. Straining their leashes, they yelped at Napoleon, but Napoleon trotted straight ahead.

Dinah and Olive reached the corner at Van Buren Street. Olive whispered: *"Achtung!"* Attention. "Rich man coming."

Did Napoleon hear? Dinah watched the dog kneel forward and cover his nose with a paw, as if he hated the smell of Chicago's rich people. Olive had taught him that trick. Dinah smiled.

As she stepped aside, Dinah decided the man striding toward her was probably not a millionaire. Millionaires rode those fancy carriages drawn by sleek, fat horses. However, this man was rich enough: well dressed, well fed, and well met.

With a moan, she threw herself across the man's feet and made him stumble. Her back ached from her long workday; she felt as if she wanted to lie there forever. But that, of course, was impossible. As the man leaned over Dinah, Olive darted up.

Dinah crawled to her knees. "Sorry, sir," she muttered, head down. He mustn't see her face.

Shawl covering her head, she stood and limped along

Van Buren Street toward the lake. Behind her she heard Olive speak angrily. "You, you, how dare you. You knock her down!"

The man stuttered, "I believe . . . I do believe she—"

Without glancing behind, Dinah knew that Ben Schaffer had thrown the stone on time. She heard the man call, "My hat!"

She heard his footsteps as he ran after his rolling derby. Testing the wind with a finger, she sensed that the breeze had carried his hat south. Good. That meant Napoleon hadn't been needed. She felt the thrill of a successful humbug, but at the same time she felt a stab of shame.

A hand signal brought Napoleon to her side, and she stumbled out to Lake Michigan's breezy shoreline, where the air was clean and smelled of fresh seaweed floating at the foamy water's edge. The others would meet her there. They couldn't be seen together right away.

Napoleon sniffed a bloated fish. As he began to nibble it, Dinah squatted on the damp sand and drew her long skirt around her ankles. Her joking father liked to ask what the lake said to the lakeshore. She would giggle and answer, "Nothing. It just waved."

He would ask, "Was it beautiful?" He always looked for beauty, but not just the kind you see with your eyes. Her father, a union organizer, felt the struggle for justice was beautiful, too. The calm lake whispered of beauty to Dinah now, and she sighed.

Why wasn't her father more practical, more down-to-earth? He was a dreamer seeking the good, the true, and the beautiful; but it was hard for Dinah to notice beauty when she was hungry. She watched Napoleon eat the dead fish, sand and all. She was pleased. His stomach was as strong as a tin tub. Some dogs of working people had ribs that showed like porch railings, but not her dog.

A year ago Dinah and Olive had rescued Napoleon when his tail got chopped off. They had seen men throw him out of the metal-works plant at McCormick's Reaper Factory, where their fathers had worked. The bloody pup must have followed someone inside.

His chopped six-inch tail had hung from a one-inch stump. Olive had cut the skin; Dinah had torn her petticoat to make a bandage; and the grateful puppy had become their loyal pet.

After finishing the fish, Napoleon flushed a prairie hen off a nest and ate her eggs. Dinah's stomach churned painfully as she watched him. She grew so dizzy, she stumbled up the shore and sat. Leaning against an oak tree, she began to think.

It was Thursday, two days before the Saturday march for the Eight-Hour Day. She, her mother, and her father would march with thousands this May 1 demanding a shorter workday. Thousands were out of work and were hungry. Her father worked sixteen hours a day on his new job. With an Eight-Hour Day and fair wages, two men could have jobs; two families could have food.

She frowned. I hope the humbug's a good one, she thought, hugging her knees. Then we won't have to do it again for a few days. That spring there had been weeks of lockout and then the McCormick blacklist for her father and his friends. Ten weeks in all, and for three of those weeks they had almost starved; for the other seven, the children had done humbug once or twice a week.

Remembering Josef, Dinah moaned.

Before they began humbug, Josef Schaffer, six, had been ill with fever and weak from hunger. The day before he died, Dinah had played rolling a ball from her bed to his. He hadn't learned English, and she spoke little German, but their play hadn't needed words. They were friends.

The next day Josef lay staring until, eyes and mouth open, without a whimper, he died. That day as she wiped a tear, Dinah promised herself no one else in the family would die. Humbug had been the answer.

"Desperate times call for desperate measures," their priest had said. Dinah wasn't sure he would approve of their "desperate measures," but it was all they knew to do.

At last Olive warbled—her signal—and Dinah whistled in return. Running toward Dinah, Ben carried a narrow loaf of unwrapped bread. With a yell, Dinah lunged, tore an end off the bread, and bent over her knees to chew it.

She swallowed a lump of the crust, gulping so fast it scratched her throat. She ran and knelt by the lake, where she slurped water, then chewed more bread, stuffing it in her mouth. Turning her back to Olive and Ben, she hid three chunks of bread in her pocket.

Staggering back, she asked Olive, "What else?"

Olive wiped her lips. The bread was gone. She lifted a key high. Ben grabbed at it, but Olive dropped it in her pocket.

Ben pointed to his feet. "I can buy boots."

"That much?" Dinah asked, brushing sand off her damp skirt.

Olive nodded, then glanced away, and Dinah suspected there was something Olive didn't want to tell her in front of Ben.

Dinah turned to Ben, who worked unloading boats on the Chicago River. "Why buy shoes?" she asked, frowning.

Ben sat, rolled on his back like a porcupine, and raised both feet. Wet newspaper bulged like snake heads from holes in the bottoms of his shoes. She stared at the holes.

"Splinters and stones hurt feet in there," he said. "Two men die from gangrene. I need shoes."

Dinah nodded. Where she worked, sewing needles hurt fingers, not feet, and always at the end of their long work shift when people were tired.

Women seamstresses at their factory sewed sixteen-hour shifts. Sometimes they sewed eighteen hours or more when a shipment of shirts or gloves was needed. Because she and Olive were children, they worked only twelve hours—from seven in the morning until seven in the evening.

Ben stood and gazed down the lakeshore.

A well-dressed man strolled with a girl. The laughing girl, about Dinah's age, was dressed in a peach-colored dress with lace at her neck. Dinah straightened her back. She remembered having pretty clothes. Did that girl think she was better than Dinah because of her fancy dress?

Dinah heard the man call the girl "Rosellen."

As they walked closer, Dinah wished she could throw sand in that Rosellen girl's face. Olive and Ben stood to leave, but Dinah lingered to stare, clenching her teeth like an angry bulldog.

She bet that girl was in school. No long hours of work for her. Dinah had had to go to work two years ago, and she still missed school. Why couldn't she have fine clothes? Why couldn't she stay in school?

Turning, Dinah trudged up the sand to follow Olive. "What else?" she asked in a low voice. Ben had left.

Shaking her head, Olive said, *"Gefahr!"* Danger!

"Why?" asked Dinah.

"Last man we take money purse from?"

"Yes," whispered Dinah. Olive was the one who picked the pockets. What had she learned? How were the three of them in danger?

"Pinkerton detective."

The Pinkertons, killer sharks for hire! Pinkertons were worse than the police. Dinah frowned as she walked a safe distance ahead of Olive on their way to Chicago's north division. Could they find another way to pay for food for the family? They had to. Humbug was becoming too dangerous.

CHAPTER TWO

When Dinah and Olive reached the north division's saloons and shops, the streets smelled of home. Dinah's nose tingled from the smell of droppings from delivery-wagon horses, and the scent of warm beer from saloons. Here no wealthy lady would frown at Dinah, because everyone was poor.

The three- and four-story tenement buildings around them housed thousands. But before the girls could go to the one they called home, they had to shop for food for the family.

With money in hand, Dinah walked to a colored butcher's shop. His floor was covered with layers of blood-soaked straw. She asked for entrails, a big amount of meat for little money. He reached into a barrel, and flies swarmed off the fatty intestines. Dinah batted flies from her face.

"Could you rinse them out, please?" she asked. By this time of evening women were in line to get water. One pump in the alley provided water for everyone in the neighboring buildings. There would be no way she could wash the meat herself.

The butcher used a hose to wash the entrails, chopped them on his bloody butcher board, and wrapped the heavy clump in newspaper. "Thank you," Dinah said, proud to have bought meat. It felt good in her arms.

While Dinah bought meat, Olive shopped for vegetables. The grocer was Austrian and treated Olive to the best. Olive had told Dinah about her farm in a sunny valley beneath snowcapped mountains in Austria. Chicago-born, Dinah couldn't imagine a mountain, but she knew Olive could choose good vegetables.

Both grocer and butcher knew the girls because the men attended anarchy meetings. These were held at the back of the saloon on the first floor of the girls' tenement.

Olive and Dinah met in the alley behind the building that held their fourth-floor room. Napoleon wagged his short tail, and his whole rump moved. Dinah smiled.

"*Achtung!* Walk fast," Olive said, passing Dinah. Olive was impatient with the new immigrants who crowded the streets and alleys, many of them with no place to call home. "They should go back," she told Dinah. "Not enough work for them." It was true, Dinah thought. Like moths to a flame, twice as many people were outside factories begging for jobs as there were people inside the factories working.

Dinah nodded to Olive and plunged into a crowd of immigrants. As she passed, men and women rose from sitting against the wooden building. The women in long skirts wore scarves tied under their chin; the men wore caps and woolen suits. Other homeless people huddled around trunks of belongings.

When the girls climbed the outside wooden stairs, about thirty people followed like hungry sheep following young shepherds. Olive turned and yelled, "Go back down. We not have for you. Our own family must be feeding."

The people squatted on the stairs like vultures waiting. When Dinah glanced behind her, she saw them with bowls in their hands. But children's humbug couldn't feed them all. Her heart ached for them.

At the top of the stairs, Olive kicked their door open. Three little Schaffer children, as white-haired as their older sister and brother, ran up. Olive walked directly to a table in the middle of the room, but Dinah, standing in the doorway, stuffed chunks of bread in the little Schaffers' mouths and kissed their dirty faces. They were a four-, a two-, and a one-year-old. As they chewed, they tiptoed away like tiny mice.

Dinah's mother, Mrs. Mary Bell, stepped from the pantry she claimed for privacy. After all, the Bells had lived in the room first, and Dinah's father—Mr. Noah Bell—paid most of the rent. Dinah thought her mother was pretty enough to be an actress, with her long, wavy black hair pulled into a bun, and her large eyes in an earth brown face. Her papa loved beauty, all right.

How had they ended up here? Dinah frowned and tried to remember:

Her mother had told her, "And fifteen years ago in Cairo, Illinois, we owned our home. And my widowed mother here in Chicago lived over her own dressmaking shop."

The Great Chicago Fire had started the change in her family's life. Her mother said, "Your grandmother's home burned the first night of the fire, and she lost her savings and her livelihood. What were we to do with her in trouble?

"When we moved to Chicago, money was good," she told her. "And with all the rebuilding, folks had jobs for decent pay."

They moved three years before Dinah was born. Her father had owned a blacksmith shop in Cairo. Because he knew about metal works, he got a job at the McCormick Reaper Factory. Mr. Cyrus McCormick Sr. and his brother were reasonable men. Their employees had had one of the first metalworker unions in the city, Molders Union Local 23. Under the senior McCormick, the workers' lives had been good.

But two years ago old Mr. McCormick had died. His young son, Mr. Cyrus McCormick Jr., took over the company. He kept cutting wages and making the men work longer hours. When her father could no longer pay rent and buy food, too, her mother went to work.

That was when her parents moved from a house into that tenement room. Worse still, her mother had an accident on her job, and her grandmother died. "And our savings went to give my mother a decent burial," said Dinah's mother.

It seemed good times had ended then.

Not only that, but the number of people in Chicago had increased rapidly—one hundred and twenty-five thousand immigrants in the past year alone. Now Dinah looked around the crowded room and sighed.

Hands on hips, Mrs. Bell stared at her daughter. "Well, it's about time. And where have you been? And you know you have more to do, don't you?"

Head down, Dinah walked in. Her mother always fussed at her. She was pretty, like her mother, but she hoped she would never fuss like her mother.

The room held three families joined into one, seventeen people in all. Each family had a corner, and children played in the middle. Two windows opened onto a street of maple trees whose leaves were rosy tipped from springtime.

Dinah opened her meat on the table.

"And don't you know to close the door?" asked Dinah's mother. "You weren't born in a barn like these white riffraff. We have aristocracy in our veins."

"Mama, don't say that." Dinah felt her face grow warm.

"Say what? That we weren't born in a barn?"

"You know." For a moment Dinah covered her face.

"Why're you treating me like this?" Her mother's voice grew shrill. "Who do you think you are?"

"Mama," said Dinah softly, "don't call people riff-raff." She picked wet newspaper off the meat.

"Look at that door. You still didn't close the door. And you think you're big enough to tell me what to say, do you?"

Dinah turned to close the door. In the hall children

from other rooms on their fourth floor—the Dahls, the Larsons, and the Peersons—children of Swedish immigrants, stood staring at the meat. Their working families could pay rent but had little left for food.

Dinah said, "It won't be long," and closed the door gently.

"It will be long. And the dead wagon took your father's friend Otto Ruttenberg today. His wife, Gretchen, already dead, and three little orphan girls out there to die." Dinah saw tears in her mother's eyes.

"Mr. Ruttenberg's dead, Mama?"

"Dead and stiff as a broom." Her mother's voice softened. "All the decent men are dying, Dinah. We have to take care of your father. Something bad has happened to him, I can feel it in my bones." Her voice cracked, and she dabbed her eyes.

Her mother's bones always foretold tragedy; but Dinah felt sad about Mr. Ruttenberg. Olive's eyes, too, brimmed with tears. Gretchen and Otto Ruttenberg had been Austrian immigrants, as the Schaffers were. Dinah glanced around.

Olive's father, Mr. Schaffer—with a black armband for grief—was asleep on the floor by his trunk. Mrs. Schaffer, wearing black mourning, sat on the floor mending clothes and hugging her one-year-old. With Josef dead, there were now five Schaffer children.

The other corner belonged to the Polish Zagorski family—father, mother, and five older children who stared hungrily at Dinah. One sucked the handle of her soup cup.

No one in the room spoke Polish, and the Zagorskis

spoke no English, but Polish-speaking people from Milwaukee Avenue came by to visit and translate for them. Whenever Mr. Zagorski got a job, he gave money to Dinah's father. The three families were not a likely group to live together as *family*, but the men—Mr. Bell, Mr. Schaffer, and Mr. Zagorski—had worked side by side at McCormick's Reaper Factory.

Dinah went to the wood-burning stove. Her meat slid into the pot that sat there, sloshing boiling water over the sides. With a cup Dinah dipped hot water into another pot. Most of Olive's vegetables would be added later, but now Olive chopped garlic and onions to season the soup. Soon it would smell good.

They had been lucky to find that ten-gallon pot. Last winter a family had frozen in the alley, and they had left a trunk. Other people took clothes from the trunk, but Dinah took the large pot. Now with money from humbug she felt responsible for filling it every evening. She hated doing humbug, but she loved being a provider.

The first time Dinah stole money, it was because she had fainted from hunger. When she recovered and found a crowd around her, she felt a small leather purse in the pocket of a man who had bent down to help her up. Without thinking, she had snatched it, and hid it in her skirt pocket.

What she had done had frightened her, but Olive had approved. The ten dollars in the purse had fed the family well for a week. Now the adults expected food daily, and none of them asked where the children got the money.

Even Dinah's father had disappointed her. He didn't seem to care how the children bought food, as long as there was food to eat. Sometimes she wished the grown-up people would stop them, but then, of course, the family might starve.

To make it easier, they had practiced. She and Olive had fun picking Ben's pockets. Sometimes he really didn't feel it, but when he did, he hit them. "Police catch if you steal like that," he would say. And they were more careful next time.

Olive was better than Dinah at picking pockets, and she could scold in German, which really angered the rich men. So their humbug went this way: Dinah stumbled into the man, Olive picked his pocket and scolded, and Ben added the last distraction while they got away. In case they were suspected, Napoleon would come at Olive's signal to bark.

Once Dinah had told Father O'Connor about three children who stole to feed a large family. With a sigh he had said, "Desperate measures for desperate times."

Dinah's mother sighed now. "And why did you take so long? I've been sitting here wasting firewood and boiling water all evening. Why don't you children ever think of anyone else?"

Dinah crawled under the table and lay on her sleeping pad. Her aching back felt good against the hard floor. What would it be like to work for eight hours, instead of twelve or sixteen? Workers were always so weary.

Her bed was the safest place in the room because there no one could step on her, but her mother walked over and nudged her with a foot.

"And you have to go back out because your father

didn't come home, and he's gone. And they probably found out about him." Mrs. Bell began to cry.

Fear gave Dinah a jolt. It was possible that her papa's new employer, who didn't know he was a member of both the Knights of Labor and the metalworker's union, had found out about him. What would that mean?

Papa hadn't come home? That had never happened before. For a second Dinah wanted to get up and hug her worried mother; but her mother smelled unwashed, and there was stink from the yellow-stained bandages on her arm nub.

Holding her arm nub high, Dinah's mother said, "Your father may be lost and I can't work. I was the fastest worker they ever had. But once my arm was gone, they kicked me out without so much as a farewell." She wept loudly now.

Suddenly Dinah giggled, and she saw Olive covering a snicker. Sometimes they had to leave the room when something seemed funny, because the grown-ups grew angry about their laughter.

"And," said her mother, "watch out for the needles. But most of all watch out for that cutting blade at the factory. First I lost my thumb, and then my hand, and then my arm."

Dinah had heard this every day for over a year, ever since her mother's accident at the sewing factory. But now Dinah had to find her father. If he had a meeting, he always came home before going back out. What had kept him tonight?

She peeked in the pantry, where her parents slept on

a cot. For some reason she remembered when they had had a big bed and she had been little. Sometimes she had slept in the middle between her father and mother. They would reach over her and hold hands, and she had felt warm and safe.

Now on her father's side of the cot, Dinah touched his wooden rosary, which had a Coptic cross. Beside that, there was a candle stump.

I'll take them, she thought. I may need them.

She also slipped matches off the stove and put them in her pocket with the rosary and the candle. She stepped out the door and walked down stairs lined with people. It hurt to know that they were hungry and homeless.

Among them she recognized the three little brown-haired Ruttenberg girls, their eyes swollen and red. Now they had lost both mother and father. What would happen to them?

Where is *my* father? Dinah wondered with a tingle of fear. If something had happened to him, what would happen to her?

CHAPTER THREE

When Dinah reached the bottom of the tenement steps, she heard someone speaking at a meeting. Anarchists had rented the back of Mr. Meinrad Vonbusch's first-floor saloon that night. She peeked in the room.

"March with us Saturday for the Eight-Hour Day," the person was saying. "More jobs, more pay. We need to make a new free society with no government. Equal rights. An exchange of equal services and products. Peace and plenty for all."

People cheered.

Dinah shook her head because she agreed with her father that greed would ruin an anarchist's world, too. Her father said that unions could be watchdogs to force owners to share their profits. He thought a capitalist society fostered ambition.

She loved to hear her father speak at meetings. How proud she felt when people, colored and white, clapped for him. He'd beg colored people not to take wages lower than whites', undercutting the unions. And he insisted on good working conditions. He said they needed that Eight-Hour Day simply to be human.

Inside the meeting room, wall candles flickered. Dinah searched for the familiar broad shoulders, the curly black hair crowning her father's head. She caught her breath in a sob. What if he never came back? Her papa was her best friend. Sometimes on Sundays they sneaked away to fish off a pier in Lake Michigan. The best part was sitting together and waiting in silence. She sniffed.

The room smelled of dirty bodies, men and women with nowhere to wash themselves. She saw someone who knew her father, and she stepped inside.

"Pardon, Mr. Ascher, is my father here? Have you seen him?"

He shook his head to both questions.

"Thank you just the same."

Outside the meeting hall, people were busy painting signs in red and black. Dinah stared up and down the alley. The sun had set and the Chicago sky glowed orange from gaslights. Was her papa coming? Inside she heard people shuffle to stand.

"Are we united?" the speaker called. "Are we hand and heart together?"

"Yes!" they shouted.

When Dinah recognized a couple of "amens" shouted

by colored workers, she smiled. Her father had probably recruited them.

A piano led the people in singing the "Eight-Hour Day Song," Dinah's favorite. Pulling her shawl against the evening breeze, she walked down the alley and wandered along Lake Street. Her father walked home that way. By gaslight she stared at unshaven men gathered in groups. She stepped over beer bottles, wind-shredded newspapers, and handbills.

Papa, where are you? she wondered. She had met him here before. She spied two split logs that must have rolled off a wagon. Firewood. Quickly she picked them up and pulled her shawl over them. Half a block later, in the dark, she passed a man who called out.

"Is that bread?" he asked. "I ain't had nothing to eat all day." He jerked the wood and knocked her down.

Scrambling to her feet, she wrestled him for the wood and won. "You can't eat this!" Half a block farther she felt breathless and weak. At the Chicago River she leaned against a stone wall.

"Dinah Bell." A man's voice, but not her father's.

"Yes, sir." She stared into the dark.

"Your father's in trouble." The man spoke in a whisper. "They dragged him out of the factory. A woman spy told that he was on a blacklist, that he was in a union, that he was Mr. Noah Bell."

Dinah closed her eyes. The first thing she thought about was money for rent. Now they would be without her papa's wages, and it was Thursday. Saturday the rent—six dollars for the week—was due. Her father's pay was five dollars a week, and the others made up the rest. What would they do now? She worried, and then was ashamed to be thinking about the rent when her father was in trouble.

"Do you know where my father is?"

The man standing in shadows shook his head. "Go home, child. He'll return as soon as they release him. Just pray that he isn't . . . anyway, go home now."

Dinah sighed and said, "Thank you, sir."

The man disappeared, and the evening seemed even gloomier than before. Gaslights made scary shadows that seemed to clutch at her as she walked. She was nearing home when she saw a body racing toward her like a bullet.

"Napoleon!" Sitting on a factory doorstep, she laid her face on Napoleon's short fur and leaned against the door.

"Napoleon," she whispered as she hugged his warm body, "we're in big trouble. Mr. Noah Bell is out of work again."

Dinah reached in one of her deep pockets, and her father's rosary comforted her. Did God care about poor people?

"Napoleon," she said, looking around, "let's go. I'll see if Father O'Connor can help us. He's not rich."

Dinah stroked the hound dog's head. "Good dog, how did you find me?"

Napoleon sniffed her skirt.

"Can you really follow a person's scent in this big city?"

The dog wagged his rump. Dinah wondered how she

smelled. Was she both dirty and stinky? She sighed, and remembered her job to find her father.

"I name you Blackerton Detective Dog," she said, tapping the dog's head. "If Mr. Allan Pinkerton can start a Pinkerton Detective Agency, I, Dinah Bell, can start a Blackerton one. We're colored together, you know." She grinned.

Only Napoleon's teeth and pink tongue shone in the gaslight.

"With your nose and my eyes, we'll find Mr. Noah Bell." She picked up the wood. Father O'Connor lived at a yellow stone Catholic church that was close to home.

Dinah and Napoleon trudged toward it slowly, staring at soldiers guarding factory doorways, and dodging shivering beggars. Dinah hated beggars; she would rather steal than beg.

At the steps of the church rectory she stopped. All day she had eaten only a mushy apple at noon and that chunk of bread in the evening. Now the dizzy feeling returned, and her stomach cramped. She sat down, but Napoleon scampered up the steps. In the street a horse harnessed to a carriage whinnied.

"Girl, there. Who are you?" That Rosellen girl Dinah had seen at the lakeshore peeked out of the carriage. Imagine meeting her again on the same day.

"Never mind. Who are you?" Dinah asked, sitting straight, head high. She felt her face grow warm. Her heart began to beat against her ribs, and she grew breathless.

"You don't have to be poor, you know," said Rosellen. "This is America; you can be rich, too."

"How?"

"Work hard and save. My papa does."

Dinah stared at her. "We do work hard, but they don't pay us enough to live on. How could we save?"

Napoleon barked, and the rectory door opened. Two men passed Dinah—Rosellen's father and a chauffeur in a dark blue uniform who drove the carriage away.

Father O'Connor called, "Hello, Napoleon. Where are the little ladies? There you are, Dinah. Child, come in."

At his voice Dinah felt like crying, because the priest always welcomed them. He didn't seem to care if she was dirty. Since he was thirty-six, he joked that if he subtracted Dinah's age and Olive's age from his, he'd be twelve, too.

He ran down the steps and reached for her. "That gentleman just left us a bushel of bread loaves and a pot of soup. Come and eat."

Dinah hid her firewood under a bush. Rosellen's father had been generous to donate food for the hungry, but Dinah wasn't sure she wanted his charity.

"Napoleon, you come, too," the priest said with an Irish brogue tickling his tongue. He pulled Dinah by the hand. With her other hand she was fingering her father's rosary. Her father might even be home by now; but if he wasn't, he was in deep trouble.

From the doorway Dinah smelled chicken soup, and her mouth began to water. Charity food or not, she had to eat. Food would give her strength to search for her father.

CHAPTER FOUR

Dinah lifted the second helping of soup that Father O'Connor had poured for her, and gulped from her bowl. She stuffed a roll into her mouth. With fingers she picked chicken, celery, and carrots from the bottom of the bowl. Eyes closed, she chewed lovingly.

She was seated at a round table in the rectory's large kitchen. Black and white tiles reflected lamplight off the walls. Father O'Connor sat opposite her, and in the back a plump cook with straggly black hair was busy. A kettle hissed steam, boiling water for the priest's second cup of tea. Father O'Connor leaned forward.

"It was all right for your father not to give his real name to that employer. No one is ever obliged to obey an unjust law," he told Dinah. "And both the blacklist and the ironclad oath never to join a union are unjust."

At this point she noticed a spoon beside her soup bowl. She picked it up sheepishly. No wonder the cook had been staring. There was also butter for the bread, and a silver butter knife. Dinah sighed. The priest and the cook must have thought that she ate like a starving animal.

Only two years ago her family had had nice things like these, and they had lived in a house. Now they were so bad off that Dinah ate like an animal and needed to be a thief; she gave a shuddering sigh.

"Father," she said softly, "Olive, Ben, and me, we humbug money to feed the family."

The priest looked at the floor. This was what Dinah loved about Father O'Connor, he never scolded them. Once he had told her that his family was near starving in Ireland, and that he still sent money home.

"You have a right to food, you and the family. Could you go to one of the soup kitchens?" He sighed. "I know they have long lines and turn people away, but they have hot soup around noon."

"We work from seven to seven."

"That's inhumane! Workers with long hours, I don't know how they manage. Men and women always weary, staggering home. So little time to celebrate living."

The priest began to pace the floor. "But if you could steal away"—he smiled at the word *steal*—"go to the back door of the soup kitchen in the church on Washington Street. That way you won't have to stand in line. Ask for Miss Hallelujah LaSalle, and tell her I sent you."

"I don't know," Dinah said. "We could try."

"'Tis true," he said. "Companies are squeezing their labor force—fewer people, longer hours, lower pay—for higher profits for the owners."

Dinah nodded. Her father said that his color was also against his getting a job. She was ashamed to mention that.

"My father says we're wage slaves," she said.

At the words *wage slaves* Napoleon flopped on the floor in the middle of the kitchen. He rolled on his back with all four feet in the air. Dinah giggled, the cook chuckled, and the young priest exploded in laughter.

In the midst of their laughter the pastor walked in. Dinah sank back in her chair. At a snap of her fingers Napoleon rolled to his feet and hid under the round table.

"May I ask what's going on here?" the tall pastor with a bulging belly said, frowning. "Why is this dirty colored child in the rectory?"

Father O'Connor winked at Dinah and sat down. He stirred a silver tea strainer in his cup of hot water and laid it on a china saucer.

Pushing back strands of hair, the cook lifted the teakettle. "Won't you have a cup of tea, Monsignor Uzbek?"

"No," he said, staring at Dinah, "and this is not a relief station. Tell this colored child to go elsewhere."

No one spoke. Dinah wondered if she should leave. Under the table Napoleon rested his paws and chin on her knee; he seemed to feel her embarrassment. She stroked his head.

She remembered the pretty little house they had rented with her grandmother until two years ago. She had worn nice clothes to school; she had eaten meals from pretty chinaware.

Next Dinah remembered how her father's union had tried to negotiate for more pay with Mr. McCormick Jr. time and again. Her father said strikes were serious actions; the metalworkers tried to avoid a strike. But young Mr. McCormick wouldn't increase their pay, he lowered it.

When the metalworkers went on strike, they were "locked out," which meant that Mr. McCormick Jr. wouldn't let any workers back into his factory. The sixteenth of February this year was the day Dinah's father had returned with that news.

She glanced up at Monsignor Uzbek. He was saying something to Father O'Connor, but Dinah was lost in memories.

After the lockout the workers tried to help one another. Mr. Schaffer and Mr. Zagorski had lost their jobs, too, so their families moved in with Dinah's family. In fact, about fifteen hundred workers had lost their jobs and were blacklisted. Many, including the Ruttenbergs, ended up homeless and living on the streets.

Two weeks later Mr. McCormick Jr. reopened his factory with three hundred new workers, mostly immigrants and colored men desperate for work.

The next day, when union workers met to protest the newly hired people, the police clubbed them. Some police fired shots. A bullet tore the skin off her father's leg, and four people, two of them her father's close friends, were killed.

The lockout had been about ten weeks ago. Her

father's leg had healed, and he had found a new job under another name. But while the family was hungry, little Josef had died. As a result Dinah and her friends began doing humbug to feed the family.

Did Monsignor Uzbek know about these things? Dinah reached in her pocket and the rosary came to her touch. Pulling it out, Dinah gently laid it on the table.

Her father had made that rosary the first week he was out of work with a wounded leg. Knotted ribbon held the wooden beads apart, and with a penknife he had carved the African cross. He said that the Coptic cross meant to struggle with hope.

The monsignor walked over. "Has this rosary been blessed?"

"No, Monsignor," said Dinah, but she thought: My father blessed it with his prayers as he carved that cross.

"And this . . ." The monsignor stared at the cross.

"Coptic cross. You remember, Monsignor?" said Father O'Connor. He touched the top. "Here the Egyptian hieroglyphic for 'life,' and there the cross. Hermits and monks in the African desert used it. Early Christians, Monsignor."

"Oh, yes." Picking up the rosary, the pastor blessed it and tossed it on the table. He pulled a white linen handkerchief from his pocket and wiped his hands. "Now, leave," he told Dinah. Turning, he walked out of the kitchen.

She stood and folded her shawl on her arm.

"Child," said Father O'Connor, "come more often. Remember, you have the right to eat." He spoke in slow, careful words. "But other people have rights as well. Do what is just."

What is just. Dinah closed her eyes. Humbug was an injustice to the person they stole from, of course. She wanted justice, but she needed food. In her mind it was a little injustice to steal from others, a big injustice to starve to death. Josef had died weak from hunger.

There had been no "decent burial" for Josef, but he hadn't been carried away by the dead wagon, either. At night the family sneaked out to a prairie west of Chicago. Mrs. Schaffer chose a spot near a tree so she could remember where the little grave was, and in the dark the men had dug a hole.

Dressed in fancy clothes from their trunk, Josef was tumbled into the hole and covered, while Olive and her family quietly sobbed. Dinah had promised herself no one else in the family would starve.

However, she had to stop stealing. Dear God, she thought, show me how to get food without humbug! She looked up.

"Take courage, Dinah. God loves you." Father O'Connor held out his hand for a handshake.

"May I have two things?"

"How can I be of service, little lady?"

She pointed. "That bar of soap."

The cook almost ran to pick it off the dish by the sink. So broad was her smile that Dinah wondered how dirty she must look. Dinah dropped the soap, wrapped in paper, in a pocket.

"And the bread." She tossed her shawl over the entire basket of long, narrow loaves; she had people to feed.

"All of it?" asked Father O'Connor, smiling.

"Yes," she said. "Good-bye and thank you, Father." After shaking his hand, she asked, "Saturday we march for the Eight-Hour Day. Are your hand and heart with us, Father?"

The young priest's face grew ruddy. He opened his lips but didn't speak. Head down, Dinah walked toward the door.

Once outside she covered the bread with her shawl and laid the wooden logs on top. All the way home people grabbed the wood, thinking it was bread, then stepped aside frowning.

As she and Napoleon walked into her alley, Dinah heard drunken singing from the saloon. Homeless immigrants trying to keep warm stood by barrels of flames.

Moving quickly to the area behind her tenement, Dinah handed loaves of bread to the startled women. One woman laughed aloud as she woke her children. Luckily the two dozen loaves were perfect for her end of the alley, and Dinah hoped other women wouldn't find out.

Wood and empty basket in hand, she dragged herself up the four flights of stairs. From outside her door she heard voices fussing in German, and one snorer. She opened the door.

"And where have you been? Selfish girl, wouldn't you know I was worried? Where's your father?" Her mother was the only person Dinah had ever known who began talking with "and."

Without answering, Dinah went to the wood-burning stove. She set the wood on a pile and peeked in the soup pot. It was empty. Her mouth dropped open, and she stared. Frantic, she searched for her bowl. It, too, was empty. Her mother was silent now. Dinah stared across the candle on the table into her mother's eyes.

"I hate you," she whispered, making fists of both hands. "I might as well not have a mother." Her scalp felt prickly, and she began to sweat. "What's wrong with you, that you couldn't save food for your only child?"

No one in the family—neither her mother, nor Olive, nor Ben—had saved her a bowl of soup. But Dinah stole for the family. She fetched water, bought firewood, bought food, paid doctor bills. However, no one had saved her a spoonful of soup.

If she hadn't eaten at the church rectory, she would have gone hungry. She had been weak enough to stop breathing, she thought. Like Josef, she might have died.

Things are going to change, she decided. I have to be responsible for myself.

CHAPTER FIVE

Friday morning, still angry about the soup, Dinah rose earlier than usual. She hadn't told her mother about her father, and since she was still angry with her mother, she decided not to. As she dressed, she wondered how she could find out where he was, and how she could free him.

When Dinah left the room, Olive ran down the steps behind her. "About last night I sorry," she said. "Swedes came in to fill bowls. We feed some immigrants on stairs."

They fed some of those on the stairs? Dinah's heart leaped with pride. We children filled the soup pot so full, she thought, hungry children and their parents all ate.

Her mother had ladled out the soup well after all. Her father would say that it was beautiful to feed people—to share their food with the hungry. No wonder Dinah's

bowl had gone empty. Even though her mother complained about the people eating, she had stretched the
food to feed as many as possible. Dinah felt ashamed of
her anger at her mother.

At the alley pump Dinah pulled out her soap and
rolled up her sleeves. She couldn't stay angry with Olive
for long, either; Olive would have to help her find her
papa. She lathered her hands, then passed the soap.

"Soap? Where you steal from?"

Dinah asked, "What kind of person steals soap?"

"Dirty crook," said Olive. They both giggled.

Dinah washed her face and arms. How nice to see the
dirt rinse off, and Olive's clean face was startling. Olive
was pretty! Before washing, Olive had seemed as dirty as
a coal miner; now her rosy cheeks and blue eyes were
shining. With a sigh Dinah wrapped the soap and put it
in her pocket. Her life was already changing.

When she reached the sewing factory, Dinah waited
for Olive to catch up. "As soon as you hear church bells
for noon, leave. Pretend you have to go to the outhouse,
but keep walking. I'll meet you on Lake Street."

Olive stared at Dinah. "What humbug we doing now?"

Dinah shook her head, and they walked in. She
wouldn't tell Olive about the soup kitchen until she
was sure they could get food. She didn't want Olive to
be disappointed.

At the sewing factory Dinah and Olive joined about
two hundred women and girls on the first floor. They sat
in rows at foot-treadle sewing machines, elbow's width
apart. Attendants brought shirts or gloves or spats to be
stitched, and took away the finished bundles.

On the top floor women used machines to cut cloth. These machines were dangerous. That was how Dinah's mother had lost part of her thumb, then to keep her from dying of sepsis, her hand and arm. Dinah was grateful to be on the ground floor.

She squirmed into a more comfortable position. She had to sit on the wooden chair for twelve hours, but while she worked, she would plan how to find her father.

The woman on the shift before her had been careless; Dinah straightened a loose needle and tightened the screw. She felt slower than usual, as if her father's jailing had put ropes around her arms.

She took cloth for white summer gloves. Most days her sewing machine hummed, but today it groaned as she stitched in lines that weren't as neat as usual.

Shortly after eleven bells at the nearby church, Dinah heard the manager's voice and then a commotion upstairs. Women shouted, "Oh, no!"

The man's voice grew louder. Dinah heard: "Shut up, you dumb wenches. There's not one of you that can't be replaced in five minutes. You riffraff, keep your sewing machines going."

Dinah's hands began to tremble, and she slowed down.

"Child, y'all want an apple?" The colored woman behind her fed several of the young girls every day. Dinah chewed the mushy, tasteless apple as she stitched. Her neck already ached from guiding the cloth under the needle.

The manager came downstairs and called out, "I say now, keep your machines going. Girls, listen well.

"No one, I repeat, no one is allowed to walk with

those communist malcontents, that anarchist rabble, tomorrow." A woman who spoke German and Polish repeated his words.

What walk? Dinah wondered. Did he mean her papa's march for the Eight-Hour Day?

"Should workers tell owners how many hours they want to work?" The woman repeated what he had said.

"As for your men, I say, saloon keepers want them to be loafers instead of laborers."

Goose bumps rose on Dinah's arms.

"The situation is the following: Anyone leaving this sewing factory, I say, anyone leaving will lose her job." He paused. "Today is Friday. Girls, you are usually paid on Friday."

Oh, no, thought Dinah.

"This week, I say, this week you will be paid on Monday. Anyone leaving—"

The first floor broke out in moans and begging. "But the rent is due Saturday," someone called. That was true, Dinah thought; besides, she had already worked for that money, and her father had lost his week's pay. How would they manage?

Women called out and cried. One woman screamed, and fainted. Women stood.

"Leave her there. I say, sit down," called the manager. "Attendant, sit down. Any more ruckus, and you'll all be fined." The women sat.

Church bells rang for quarter of twelve. Dinah left a glove under the needle and stood slowly. Anger flickered inside her. Wage slave she was; they owned her work, but they didn't own her spirit. Here was a chance to do something beautiful. She might be dirty, smelly, and a thief, but she wasn't mean. She could be kind. Slowly, head high and defiant, she walked to kneel by the woman.

"Girl, get away from her," shouted the manager. "I say, get away."

He doesn't even know my name, Dinah thought.

Suppose this woman had been her mother? Mrs. Mary Bell, her bleeding hand in dirty rags, had walked two miles alone to reach Cook County Hospital.

From the other end of the room Olive appeared. Together they pulled the woman, with her legs dragging the floor. The aisles were so narrow they carried her sideways.

Outside they laid her under a tree, and Dinah wiped her forehead. An attendant ran out with a cup of water and ran back in. Olive splashed some on the woman's face, and the woman moaned. They helped her sit up against the tree, and Olive spoke to her in German.

"She must be all right now," said Dinah. "Let's go."

As she spoke, church bells began to ring the noon Angelus. Olive followed at a distance as Dinah walked rapidly, weaving around lines of homeless families. By the time she reached the church, she felt dizzy.

In front of the soup kitchen stood a double line of people holding bowls and waiting in sunshine. Tattered clothing waved like sad banners in the spring breeze. Women covered their heads and faces in embarrassment. Men stared, stone-faced, into space. Children whimpered, the only voices heard.

Dinah knocked at the back door. "Miss Hallelujah LaSalle," she said, and felt a blush on her cheeks. She despised beggars; now she had joined them, eating from a soup kitchen.

Miss Hallelujah was colored and pretty. Under her tan apron she wore a dress of red-and-black plaid with a black belt. "Welcome, girls, I'm so pleased to see you." She shook their hands with vigor.

"Father O'Connor sent us," said Dinah. She hated this, but she had to take care of herself and Olive. She was changing her life, but would she be able to get back into the factory?

Like a mother hen, Miss Hallelujah pulled both girls into the room. "I'll be right back," she said, hugging their shoulders. Dinah sighed. Miss Hallelujah didn't look down on them.

She reappeared carrying soup, bread, and a glass of milk. Behind her Father O'Connor, wearing ordinary shirt and pants, carried a second bowl of soup, bread, and a glass of milk.

"Milk," Dinah said, and giggled with Olive. She hadn't tasted milk in two years, or had it been three? If only the little children in the family could drink milk.

Dinah was so grateful, she made the sign of the cross and thought, Thank you, God. But Olive's face was buried in the soup bowl. Picking up the spoon this time, Dinah rapidly ate her soup and drank the milk.

She and Olive stood at the same time. "We won't get paid until Monday this week," she told Father O'Connor. "And if we march for the Eight-Hour Day, we lose our jobs and this week's wages."

"That's not fair," said Miss Hallelujah. "Maybe you don't want to march anyway?"

Not march? thought Dinah. Her father had spent years talking about the Eight-Hour Day. She remembered all the meetings where she sat under the table as he spoke.

When she was very young, she had fallen asleep at meetings. She could still feel his steps as he carried her home at midnight with her head on his warm shoulder. While Dinah pretended to sleep, her mother would fuss at her husband, but he would chuckle and hush his wife with a kiss. Where was her papa now?

Miss Hallelujah said, "What wonderful girls you are. Here." She gave each of them a roll. Dinah looked at the roll. She hated to beg, but . . .

"May I have three rolls, please?" she asked.

"Well," Miss Hallelujah said, hesitating, "yes."

Olive held out her hands for the same. "Thank you!" Like squirrels, they stuffed the rolls in their pockets and ran.

Dinah caught Olive's arm. "Now we go to the police."

Olive gasped. "Police? Are you crazy?"

CHAPTER SIX

On the way to the nearest police station, Dinah told Olive about her father's arrest. "Without his wages, or ours," she asked, "how will we pay the rent Saturday?"

"I am having two weeks' rent," Olive said.

Dinah stopped short. "Two weeks? Twelve dollars?"

"Ben not know. The man have twenty-five dollars," said Olive. "I give Ben three dollars for buying his boots. Twelve and three leave ten dollars. For a week we feed the family."

Dinah was pleased. "Good." Olive always kept the humbug money and used it well.

Dinah glanced down. "Will our clothes pass at the police station or should we try to look better?"

Olive pointed to dresses hung on a line to dry. "We steal dark blue, yes?" Olive was always ready to help.

"Other people have rights, and some lady washed those dresses," Dinah said, thinking of the priest's words. "We can steal from a store. You're right, though, dark blue would be different."

At the dry-goods store they strolled past tools, buckets, and ladders to reach the dresses in the back. "Maybe we'll only steal one, and I'll go in by myself," Dinah said.

"*Nein*, I want to go." Olive held a dress up to her chest, measuring the fit. She held another dress out to Dinah.

Suddenly Dinah stepped back, shaking her head. She couldn't do this, what had she been thinking? This would make her a real thief. There was a difference between stealing in order to eat, and stealing in order to see her father. Eating kept them from starving. "Olive, let's not," she said with a frown.

"Something wrong? You want find your father, yes?"

"I only steal to keep the family from hunger. Maybe I'll ask the way I am now."

"No one will help you when you looking dirty poor." Olive put her hands on her hips, but Dinah walked quickly to the door. Her dirty clothes weren't beautiful in the pretty sense, but they would be beautiful in the noble sense. She heard Olive dragging her feet as she followed her.

As they stepped out into sunshine, the owner called to them. "So, no shoplifting, little ladies? I was watching you." He waved his hand, and from the shadows behind a counter a policeman stepped out. He held his club in both hands and stood with feet far apart. Olive walked past him.

Dinah stared at the officer; workers called the police "bloodhounds," but could this bloodhound possibly help her?

"Sir," she asked with heart hammering, "I'm looking for my father, Mr. Noah Bell. Union man. Do you know where he is?"

"Union man?" repeated the officer. "Colored, of course. Dark like you. Curly black hair and broad shoulders. Yes, lass, he's at the station."

"Oh," and Dinah clasped her hands. "How could I get to see him, sir?" Olive lingered by the storefront.

"People don't visit union men."

"Could I call him from a window?"

"No, lass," said the policeman. "He's in an inner cell."

Dinah took a deep breath. Her father always said, Where there's a will, there's a way. "If I had stolen that dress, would you have taken me to the station?"

"Yes." And the officer smiled.

"Inside the station?"

He lowered his club and nodded. "Yes. My duty, lass."

Dinah turned. "I'll steal it." She ran back into the dry-goods store, took the dark blue dress, and ran out. Olive did the same. Outside they held the dresses high.

The officer chuckled. "What blarney! You're a lass who wants to see her papa badly."

"Yes, sir. Do you have a daughter?"

The man's face flushed, and his cheeks trembled. "My only girl, Kathleen. She would of been twelve this year. Died of whooping cough when she was a bonny lass of ten years."

The store owner quickly took the dresses from Dinah and Olive. He brushed them off and folded them across his arm.

"Come on," said the policeman. He took them by

their shoulders and pushed them ahead of him toward the station. "Sons of Patrick, this is the craziest thing I've ever done."

Olive bumped Dinah and said in a mumble, "We never walk together. Always we hiding from police. Now we ask to be arrested? *Genug.*" Enough.

Dinah understood, but she had to find her father! How could the family manage without him? He rented the room. Unlike the immigrants, he knew union leaders and important people in Chicago. He was the only man in the family who worked, and he kept everyone's spirits up.

He'd say, "When you're so far down you have to look up to see bottom, things are bound to change."

As they drew near to the Desplaines Street police station, Dinah felt grateful for the long, three-story building. The bloodhounds' house wasn't ugly, it was, in a sense, beautiful. On winter nights it was shelter for about four hundred homeless men. The police gave them each a bowl of soup and a slice of bread.

Inside the stuffy station, which smelled of human bodies, Dinah and Olive were led to a desk. Their arresting officer explained, "I'm going to take this one in the back. They were caught outside a store for stealing dresses."

The desk officer nodded, and kept reading the newspaper. A card said that his name was Mathias J. Degan.

The station seemed busy and interesting, but Dinah was breathless from fear. Olive stayed in the outer room while Dinah walked toward an iron-barred gate the policeman held open.

At the gate she whistled, and listened for an answer. Her father should have whistled back, if he had heard.

Instead, she heard a howl at the station door. Within seconds a dark body hurled itself through the gate behind her, and Napoleon jumped into Dinah's arms.

"What's this, lass?" The officer had been bumped aside.

"Our dog," said Dinah, twisting and turning to avoid his licks. With Napoleon under her arm, she walked boldly through more doors with clanging bars, and down an echoing corridor dim as a nightmare.

"Let's check for your papa here," the officer said. They reached a large, stinking cell with about twenty men inside. Two benches had men sleeping on them, and most of the floor was taken up with men sitting.

"Do you see your father?"

Dinah stared from side to side. Many of the men were familiar from union meetings at the saloon. "Please," she asked them, "have you seen Mr. Noah Bell?"

"They took Mr. Bell out," said two men at once.

"He's free," called Dinah, hugging her dog.

"No, not likely," the officer told her. "Not until after that socialist march tomorrow, lass. I suppose he's been transferred to another station." He pulled Dinah away by her shoulder.

She wanted to ask, Is my father well? Has he been beaten? She hoped he was all right.

In the front room when Dinah explained to Olive, Olive turned to the officer. "Your books, they tell where he go?"

The policeman smiled. "Sometimes, sometimes not. We don't have enough books to write up all the trouble-makers."

Napoleon wiggled in Dinah's arms. When she put him down, he ran, sniffed the gate to the jail, and barked. So Napoleon knew her father had been there. If the police had just taken him away, could her detective dog follow where he went?

CHAPTER SEVEN

As Olive and Dinah left the police station, Dinah spied the police captain they called Bulldog Bonfield. He drilled his officers in riot control to break up marches. Square of jaw, he had dark hair and a full, bushy mustache. No mistaking him, but what was he doing?

"You that see?" Olive whispered. "From bad man he take money."

The smiling man walked away. Captain Bonfield returned to the station, patting his pocket. Suddenly Dinah felt angry. Who were the bigger thieves here: those who stole for food, or those who took money to overlook crimes?

Napoleon was barking. "Olive," she said, "see if you can slip back into the factory unnoticed. The women might not tell, and the manager doesn't even know our names." Dinah looked from Olive to the dog. "I'll follow Napoleon," she said.

The dog was sniffing the curb. Stump wagging, he ran back for Dinah. Olive shrugged, and Dinah ran after Napoleon, feeling guilty because she knew Olive wanted to come.

Headed north, the dog trotted, sniffing furiously. Without that soup and milk, Dinah felt, she wouldn't have been able to keep up with him. Between Desplaines, Washington, Randolph, and Jefferson Streets they passed through Haymarket Square.

Here a tangle of farm delivery wagons filled a square large enough to hold meetings of twenty thousand people. Those meetings were in the evenings. By day, horses, carts, wagons, and buyers filled the square. Most were from German truck farms north of Chicago. This time of year they sold hay, eggs, butter, and chickens, along with vegetables and apples from cellars.

Trotting by the curb, Napoleon wove a path along the streets. His nose was sniffing like a train chugging on tracks. Turning and heading south, he left behind the district of soot-belching smokestacks. Now four- to six-story buildings lined the streets, housing offices for lawyers, doctors, accountants, and bankers. A man in a cutaway coat held the reins of a gentleman's horse-drawn buggy. Dinah glanced up, and caught her dog.

The manager of their factory was talking to a well-dressed gentleman with a gold-handled cane. With her shawl, Dinah covered her face. "Took it well, did they?" the gentleman asked.

"Oh yes, sir," said the manager. "I think that few of

the girls will dare step out. Not with their livelihood at stake, sir." He hesitated. "But, sir, if I may . . ."

"Sure." But the gentlman glanced quickly at his gold pocket watch. He clicked it closed and slipped it back into his watch pocket. With a finger, he brushed his graying mustache.

"I say, sir, the situation is that products are piling up. Could we cut back on some of the sewing girls' hours?"

"Not at all, Mr. Brown," said the factory owner. "Lay the girls off for a month."

"But, sir, they depend on their jobs. Some of their husbands aren't working, you know. And, sir, my name is Brunsweiger, Bruns-wei-ger."

The owner lifted his derby to scratch his balding head. "Don't worry about the sewing girls, Mr. Brown. Those people don't suffer, they're barely human."

The manager stepped back for a moment. He took a deep breath. "I say, sir, not many will return after a month's layoff."

"Then," said the owner, "you'll hire new girls. Women from Europe are flooding the city, begging for work. For every girl who never returns, there'll be a hundred to take her place." Without another word, he walked into the club.

Dinah stood still with Napoleon in her arms. When the factory manager had walked on, she put Napoleon down and continued following the dog. Was it true they would be laid off? What would she do then?

At the corner of LaSalle and Monroe Streets, Dinah called Napoleon back. She wanted to gaze up at a new ten-story building. They said this Chicago Home Insurance building had a framework of concrete and steel.

Only a year old, it was the tallest building in the world. They even planned to add two more stories.

Her father would ask, "What kind of ghosts haunt tall buildings?" The answer to his joke was "High spirits."

However, her father said that fifteen years ago wealthy people had rebuilt their factories and stores after the Chicago fire at the expense of others. Money in the Relief and Aid Society had been meant for ordinary people who had lost their small businesses and homes, but it had gone to men who were wealthy already. Ordinary people grew poorer, stuffed into tenements with high rents, and the rich who owned those tenements grew richer.

Dinah looked around. She was surrounded by yellow stone office buildings with marble steps and Greek columns. Here she felt small and dirty, but she kept her eyes on Napoleon. She had to find her father.

She passed a man who was saying, "Eight-Hour Day. Imagine. Ungrateful hyenas asking to work less. Not more, you hear, but less."

Dinah couldn't help thinking how lucky those men were. They could stroll the streets of Chicago on a sunny weekday afternoon, when working people couldn't.

A couple of blocks past the commercial section of the city, Napoleon began to run. Dinah tried to keep up with him. Sniffing frantically, he ran to the back door of a block-long brick building. After scratching on the door, he began to howl. With a grin, Dinah snatched him up.

"I'm proud of you," she whispered. Her detective dog had led her to her father. This was where they had taken him!

CHAPTER EIGHT

After she learned that her father was at the Twelfth Street police station, Dinah returned to the sewing factory. Across the room Olive was busy at her machine.

"Where have you been, child?" an attendant asked.

"To the outhouse," Dinah said, sliding into her seat.

When she had sewn two gloves, Dinah reached behind her and took the hand of her apple friend. She slipped one of her soft rolls into the woman's hand without anyone noticing.

That evening, when she and Olive finished at seven o'clock, she was so tired she found herself stumbling. But she had worked only twelve hours. Others would work three or four hours more.

Dinah arrived home to find her mother moaning and hugging her injured nub. "And when I passed the factory and you weren't in your seat, I was so worried. Are you all right? And where were you?"

Dinah put her arms around her mother. I forgive you for not saving me any soup, she thought, you had so many mouths to feed. She whispered, "I went to where they're holding Papa."

"You know? And why didn't you tell me? Is he all right? And you haven't told me anything."

"Mama, someone said that the police took Papa from the furniture factory. The managers found out he was Mr. Noah Bell. First he was at the Desplaines Street police station, but now he's been taken to the Twelfth Street station."

"And I'll just go visit him, and I told him so—" Mrs. Bell stopped. "They don't much allow union men's wives to visit, and did they even admit they had him?"

"Kind of." According to Napoleon, she thought.

"And what do you mean by 'kind of'?" Mrs. Bell began to cry. "How do you think I'm supposed to feel, and my husband's been missing for two days?"

"They say they're holding some union men until after the march tomorrow," said Dinah. She felt like crying, too.

"Do they think that by holding Mr. Noah Bell they'll stop the colored workers from marching? No, they won't. The coloreds will march. And I wanted to march with my husband."

Dinah's mother took a deep breath. She clenched her fist. "And I want to raise my nub of an arm, and I want to let the world see . . ."

Dinah sighed. It was always the same with her mother.

That night the family ate well at the expense of the Pinkerton detective. The girls bought flour to thicken a soup into stew, and Dinah's mother made biscuits.

The next morning Dinah awoke early. After dressing, she wondered: how could she free her papa? Arms hugging her knees, she sat watching roaches crawl over people. Every once in a while a child would brush a roach off, but mostly folks slept quietly.

Two of the Zagorski boys, about ten and eight years old, were awake also. They couldn't speak English, but they shined shoes, and paid for matches and shoestrings for the family. Dinah smiled, and they smiled back.

She felt excited. Today was Saturday, May 1, the beginning of the Eight-Hour Day. Her father had been rallying people for two years; and when she freed him, he could march.

Several unions had gone on strike, and some companies had already given their workers an Eight-Hour Day. In fact, federal and Illinois law said the workday was eight hours, but no one enforced it. Her father said the law needed some teeth in it.

Teeth. Strength. She had eaten at noon and at night yesterday, strength for her search. By church bells she knew it was only four thirty in the morning, and she didn't start work until seven. Police stations were open day and night. Dinah stood up.

I'm going to spring my father from the bloodhounds' den, she thought, and then he can march. As she straightened her shoulders, she felt good, strong, beautiful. She tiptoed out the door. At the bottom of the steps Napoleon, who slept in the alley, joined her. Although morning was only a blush of pink in the east, and the streets were gloomy, she passed lamplighters turning off the street-lights. This time she knew her way well.

Instead of following the police wagon route, she and Napoleon walked straight to the police station. First she strolled around staring at the windows. Did his cell look out onto the street? She felt the rosary in her pocket. Wouldn't it be wonderful if she could hand it to her father?

A policeman in the doorway frowned when she circled the building the second time. Olive had warned her about being obvious. Who wouldn't notice a colored child with a brown sausage dog? Why hadn't she made Napoleon hide? Dinah sighed. She wasn't good at sneaking.

All right, she would be truthful. I'm going to spring my papa honestly, she thought, her shoulders back and head high.

Sitting on the curb, she combed her thick hair, braided it, and wound the braid around her head like an ivy wreath. Stuffing her comb in a pocket, she ate a dry roll. This time when she strolled up to the station door, she walked in.

The front room was filled with desks, benches, chairs, and sadness. The plastered walls were smudged. A bucket and mop stood by a barred door. The wooden floors had just been mopped, and the room reeked of brown soap. However, Dinah suspected the room had smelled even worse before.

"I'm here to take Mr. Noah Bell home," she told the officer at the desk. She carried Napoleon wrapped in her shawl.

"No visitors. Step aside." The policeman hadn't even glanced up at her. As he turned the page of the newspaper, she noticed that a rabbit's foot hung from his key chain.

"I'm not here to visit him, sir," she said. "I will walk home with him. Now, thank you."

"Who?"

"Mr. Noah Bell."

The officer glanced at a list. "Labor troublemaker?"

She was getting somewhere, she thought. "Union member for justice, sir."

Looking up, the policeman snorted. "What justice? No, he won't be released today."

Well, her honesty hadn't worked; how about humbug? The officer wore a rabbit's foot. She took a deep breath. "Does it say that he's a sorcerer?"

He stared at her. "What kind of sorcery?"

"African. They cast spells on people who're cruel to them."

"No one here is cruel." The policeman's voice grew loud. "We maintain law and order, that's all."

Napoleon growled from deep in her shawl. Dinah worried; she didn't want him to bark.

"What was that?" asked the officer, looking around.

"Sir?"

"I heard a . . . sound."

"Could be my papa. He's an African sorcerer and has powers. I'm sure by now he knows I'm here."

"What's your name?"

"Dinah Bell, but I can't do sorcery like my father. The gift wasn't passed to me."

"What kind of gift?" The man lowered his voice and looked around. Except for the policeman outside the door, he was alone. Puffs under his eyes made Dinah think that he had been on duty all night. She squeezed Napoleon; this time he whined.

"Are you sure you didn't hear something?" the officer asked.

"Sir? I said my father wants to see me. His spirit may be calling."

The policeman stood. For a moment he stretched as if he was stiff. "Let me go see this prisoner," he said.

As he pushed his chair aside, Dinah reached in her pocket. "Give him this, sir. It'll protect you."

He tossed it in his hand. "'Tis a rosary." A brogue crept into his speech. "What kind of cross is that?"

"From North Africa. The top is the Egyptian hiero-glyph meaning 'life.' The lower part is the Christian cross. Desert sorcerers used the cross for . . ." She couldn't think of what to say. "They weren't sorcerers," she said, "they were Christian desert hermits. Holy men."

Now the policeman looked terrified. As he stared at the rosary, one of his eyes crossed. He blinked it straight. "What did they use it for?"

Dinah took a deep breath to keep from giggling. "Besides prayers, I can't tell, sir. My father may tell you."

Holding the rosary away from his side, the officer picked up his keys and walked away. Napoleon was wig-gling. He didn't want to be held, so she put him down. Bending over, she said, "Stay," and pointed to her feet. Napoleon lay at her feet and closed his eyes. Still sleepy, she thought.

While the officer was gone, she tried to peek at the piles of paper on the desk. Olive had taught her how to read upside down. She simply read the little words first, then worked on syllables in the longer ones. Dinah used her skills now.

MEET WITH MILITIA.

PINKERTONS ON ROOFTOPS. ARMED.

COLT NAVY REVOLVERS, WINCHESTER RIFLES, REMINGTON BREECH-LOADING RIFLES.

ARM THE . . . She couldn't read the word.

The policeman returned. "Your father sends his love, and he kept the rosary. He says he's well cared for. Seems he got fired because he was on the McCormick blacklist."

He nodded to Dinah. "You can leave now."

She stood, feeling the warmth of Napoleon at her feet. She felt so helpless; so close to her father, but she couldn't free him after all. The officer picked up a pen and dipped it.

"Leave. Now!" he said.

With a half turn, Dinah stooped to pet Napoleon. What else could she do? The officer had locked the jail door. At least her father knew she had been there. She loved him so much, her dear papa. Did he realize that this was Saturday, May 1?

When she straightened up, she read the policeman's boldly printed upside-down words: NOAH BELL DANGEROUS. REMOVE HIM AT ONCE.

CHAPTER NINE

As Dinah walked home that Saturday morning, she wanted to cry, because it seemed her father was in worse trouble, and all because of her. By now the sun was shimmering out of Lake Michigan, warming the chilly spring air, but it didn't make her feel any better. Still, she had her work to do, and she'd better get back home.

When she passed a grocery store, she noticed that the delivery man had crates of round cartons. "Good morning," she said. "What's in those round cartons, sir?"

"Oatmeal," said the man. "It comes sealed in a box now."

Dinah licked her dry lips. Oatmeal would feed the family's children and the adults, too. She stared at the round cartons. The delivery man lifted the crate to his shoulder, then set it down again. "Would you like some oatmeal?"

"Yes, sir." But she hated herself for begging.

He handed her one round carton, then added another. "I'll pay for these," he said. "And give the Peersons my regards."

"I will, I will," she said, hugging the boxes in her shawl. He knew the Swedish family on the fourth floor, knew that she lived there, too. This hadn't been accepting charity. Every evening she fed the Swedes, and this was paying her back—an exchange of product for service, like the anarchists preached. She skipped a step, feeling happier.

Later, as she and Olive walked down the alley, Dinah told about her early-morning visit to the police station.

"*Unglaublich.*" Unbelievable. Olive sighed. "I should been there, then situation be better." Before they reached the street, she asked, "Why you not following your father?"

"Follow?"

"Yes, they say to remove him. Why you not following?"

"I never thought about it."

"Let that teach you. Next time carry me with you."

"Yes, Olive." It was true, they were a team. Sometimes Dinah, who was bold, had ideas; but it was Olive, who was shy, who made them work.

Separating, they walked to the factory on different sides of the street. At the door Olive caught up and asked, "What you doing? Today Saturday. You march today?"

Dinah frowned. Sometimes Olive made her angry, always waiting to see what she was going to do. "Why ask me? I don't know." Dinah turned away, but she saw Olive put her hands on her hips.

"I ask because you here for many grandparents. You take care of us Schaffers. We are new in America, not yet three years from our mountain valley." A sob caught in Olive's throat. "I ask again, you march today?"

All these months Dinah had looked forward to the march for the Eight-Hour Day, but her father's arrest had dampened her zeal. He couldn't march. Besides, she might be the only person in the factory to leave. Of course, if she left, Olive would go with her. But could both of them afford to lose their jobs? What should she do?

"I don't know," she said to Olive in a whisper.

Inside at her machine the attendant handed her a pile of shirt collars to stitch. Dinah liked them better than gloves. She sewed them inside out, clipped the tips, and turned the collars to topstitch. Other seamstresses would stitch the collars onto the shirts.

Dinah had a big decision to make. If she marched today, she would lose her job. Those three dollars a week had paid her mother's doctor bills, and had helped with firewood and food. Now they might be needed for rent, too. On the other hand, this march was important. Her father said: "Power for the poor lies in marches and strikes."

All morning Dinah wondered.

At eleven bells on the church tower, she glanced around; she had decided to risk everything and make her papa proud. He would march if he were free, and recruit others, too. Head down, Dinah spoke softly to the sewing women near her.

"Today working people will march for the Eight-Hour Day." Dinah went on, "The rich are not willing to share their profits, but we poor are willing to share our jobs. Will you march?"

Creeping on hands and knees, Dinah went up and down the rows, repeating the words. More than half of the women didn't understand English. Some elderly women stared at her as if she were crazy. Dinah shook her head. Was it any use?

At the next row, Dinah met a crawling Olive, who was following her and repeating Dinah's words in German. Dinah glanced back, and some of the women were smiling at her. Maybe some were hearing after all. She stood and headed for the stairs.

At the top, the manager stopped her. "What do you think you're doing?"

Dinah held her stomach. *"Unglaublich, unglaublich."*

He muttered, "A black German?" and let her pass.

He doesn't speak German or recognize what floor I belong on, she thought. I've worked downstairs for almost two years, and he doesn't know my face.

The manager also hadn't noticed when she and Olive had slipped out to the soup kitchen, and no one had told. It seemed that as long as the seamstresses got the quota done for the day, the manager didn't care.

Upstairs, as she crept between the cutting-board tables, she talked. Soon she heard Olive right behind her.

Church bells rang eleven thirty, then quarter of twelve. Back at her sewing machine, Dinah finished her last collar and stood up. Ready to march, she raised her chin.

I am noble, she thought, touching her braid and thinking of the Greek statue; but when she remembered their humbug and looked at her dirty dress, she lowered her face and sighed.

Wait a minute, she told herself, I provide food for the family, for neighbors, and for homeless immigrants. She stood tall again.

With trembling legs she circled the factory room, taking the longest path to the door. When she reached the door, she heard a scraping of chairs behind her. One by one the sewing machines whirred to a stop, and women tramped out of the sewing factory.

Side by side and grinning, Dinah and Olive led their own parade to join the march for the Eight-Hour Day. Dinah glanced around nervously. She hoped they wouldn't bump into anyone they had stolen from. One day, she thought, someone will catch us and call for police.

Olive asked, "What you call a dog with no legs?"

"No legs?" Dinah shook her head.

"No matter. Dog won't come anyway." Olive began giggling. Dinah was surprised, then laughed until her side hurt.

As they walked down Lake Street, they passed Clinton Street, where her mother stood waiting, and the family joined them. East–west streets leading to Michigan Avenue were thick with people, shoulder to shoulder, joining the march. A Bohemian band squeezed in front of the sewing factory seamstresses, and their music soon had everyone singing.

When they reached Michigan Avenue, Dinah saw

workers—colored and white—homeless families, immigrants, and union members from one end of the street to the other.

"No end," called Olive. "Everyone marching." Breezes blew skirts and banners, the sun was shining. Dinah nodded; her father would call this beautiful.

Her mother bared her sore nub and held it up in the sunlight. "And this is what they did to me. They chewed me up, and they spit me out," she called.

Sunshine might help heal her nub, thought Dinah. She remembered Grandmother Sally. Whenever Dinah had had running sores on her mosquito bites, her grandmother had scrubbed them and made Dinah sit in the sun to heal.

Clerks cheered and waved from windows of commercial buildings, while wealthy people stood on the sidewalks frowning. Dinah stared at their rich clothes, including one dress in lavender, her favorite color. She wondered what those people were thinking.

She thought she saw the wealthy girl from the lakeshore. At first Dinah pulled her shawl over her face; but when she peeked through it, Rosellen was staring straight at her. Tossing her shawl back, Dinah squeezed over to the curb, and Rosellen came to meet her. For a moment, face-to-face, they stared at each other. "March with us," said Dinah, waving her hand toward the marchers.

"No. You're nothing but troublemakers."

"That's true," Dinah said, nodding. "But that's not why we're marching."

"And Dinah come back," her mother called.

Dinah took a deep breath. "Thank your father for the soup, but tell him we don't want his charity. We want an honest day's pay for an honest day's work. An Eight-Hour Day."

As they pushed on in the snail-slow line of march, Dinah climbed up a light post. She couldn't find the beginning or end of the march. Michigan Avenue had rows of people marching arm in arm as far as she could see in both directions. Banners snapped in the breeze, signs dipped and turned as if they were dancing in the sunny air.

There were signs for furniture makers—her father's last job—machinists, gas fitters, plumbers, bricklayers, plasterers, butchers, toy makers, carpenters, shoemakers, printers, clerks.

Dinah's mother pulled her down from the light post. "And your father worked organizing this march ever since the 1884 convention, but he didn't get to march after all his work."

Dinah wormed herself over to Olive, who said, "*Achtung!* Up on roofs, see?" Olive tossed her yellow hair and pointed.

When Dinah glanced up, she saw men with guns pointed down. They were on the roofs of several buildings, and in windows, too. Guns aimed at the joyous march.

CHAPTER TEN

Ahead of Dinah a worker in the line of march called, "Look at their guns! Would they fire on women and children?"

Dinah wondered, too. By then everyone had seen the guns, but the musicians simply seemed to play their music stronger, people to sing their songs louder. The *tramp*, *tramp* sound of marching was bold, glorious, beautiful.

Her father always searched for moments of beauty. He said they happened when what was right and what was good came together. But Dinah realized that not everyone saw it the same.

The band was playing "Home Sweet Home." Dinah sang along.

"Are you in a gun club?" one marcher asked another.

"Guns are expensive. Dynamite is the great equalizer."

Dynamite? Dinah's father didn't believe in violence. Before she could react, a woman squeezed in among the sewing factory women. "Tuesday night," she said, "they're organizing sewing women at one hundred and seven Fifth Avenue. Mrs. Lizzie Holmes and Mrs. Lucy Parsons will be speaking. Remember, Tuesday, May fourth."

The woman passed along her message. Now the band near Dinah played "Rally Round the Flag." Dinah decided she'd go to that organizing meeting for seamstresses. Mrs. Lucy Parsons and Mrs. Lizzie Holmes were working for women's rights. They made Dinah proud to be a girl.

A man called, "They say we're eighty thousand strong today. How many blocks long is that?"

Dinah smiled, but her stomach hurt and she felt dizzy. When had she last eaten? As she began to worry about fainting, Olive bumped her elbow.

"*Achtung!* Your mouth opening." Olive fed her a small, juicy sausage, then a bit of bread. Dinah looked gratefully at her friend. Sometimes Olive waited for Dinah to make a decision, but Dinah depended on Olive for action.

"Mmm," said Dinah, "thank you."

"The woman bring food for a picnic," Olive said, "but with people so many, she giving food now."

"The Schaffer babies?"

"I feed. Your mama, too." Olive gave her a hard roll and squeezed away. People stared at Dinah.

I'm sorry I have to eat in front of them. They may be hungry, too. But I might faint if I don't, Dinah thought as she stuffed her mouth with the roll.

Her shoulder was squeezed, and she glanced up. "Father O'Connor," she said, "you're here!"

"Hand and heart with the poor my savior died for," he said.

He was not only there, but he was marching in his long black cassock and white Roman collar. Dinah knew her papa would have been proud to see Father O'Connor there. She had so much to tell her papa.

"Does Monsignor Uzbek know?"

Father O'Connor smiled. "He does by now." He lowered his voice. "It's important for me to be here to show that God cares. Some of these people don't believe in God, you know."

"Believe in God?" a man in overalls asked. He seemed unable to keep from speaking up. "I'm an anarchist. Call me socialist and communist, too. And my religion is this: to do justice for all, rich and poor alike."

"I see," Father O'Connor said.

"Service of humanity is my worship of God."

"I see."

The man, an organizer checking on people among the marchers, trotted away on the sidewalk. He was shaking his head.

Father O'Connor nodded and repeated, "I see."

"O'Connor," someone called. Looking back at Dinah, the smiling priest moved toward his friend.

Someone began a chant: "Rattle their bones, over the stones, they're only poor workers, whom nobody owns!"

Olive returned to Dinah's side, and uncovered a bowl of potato salad and a wooden stirring spoon. Dinah gobbled spoonfuls until her mouth was stuffed. Olive tossed her shawl over the bowl and slipped away through the crowd. Clearly she was feeding the family, but where had the salad come from?

Behind them someone screamed out in a language Dinah didn't understand. A woman leaned down. "That lady, her saying the potato salad is stolen from her son. Your friend is a thief."

Dinah nodded yes. I'm a thief, too, she thought. And I hate it. God, help me please!

She heard Olive warble. That meant she was signaling Ben, letting him know where she was. A dog howled. When Dinah whistled, Napoleon yelped his way through marching feet. Dinah picked him up and hugged him to her side. Now we're all in the march except Papa, she thought. And she began to sing when the musicians started playing the "Eight-Hour Day Song":

> "We mean to make things over,
>   We're tired of toil for naught,
>   But bare enough to live on
>   Never an hour for thought.
>   We want to feel the sunshine
>   We want to smell the flowers
>   We're sure that God has willed it,
>   And we mean to have eight hours.
>   We're summoning our forces,
>   From shipyard, shop, and mill:
>   Eight hours for work, eight hours
>   For rest, eight hours for what we will."

Dinah rubbed her cheek on her dog's warm, furry head; and she thought of how much Papa liked that song. Next they played the "March of the Workers Song."

"*Achtung!*" Ben's voice. Squeezing into the march, he caught Dinah's arm roughly. "Napoleon tell me by barking. I going by when your papa taken away in wagon going fast. He was in a bag, calling."

What did that mean? Could that be true? Dinah frowned at Ben. He shook her arm. "This from wagon he throw to me."

And Ben gave her the handmade rosary with the Coptic cross.

CHAPTER ELEVEN

Stumbling now, Dinah stared at Ben as they marched in line. Why had they put her father in a bag? Where were they taking him? She wanted to run to the place where the wagon had been. But what about her mother?

Olive squeezed up to them, and Dinah grabbed her hand. "What should we do?"

"Sunday all day we search. Now we wait."

"*Nein. Gefahr!* Now do searching," said Ben, punching Olive's shoulder.

"What they can do him?" Olive asked, shoving her brother.

Dinah didn't know who, Olive or Ben, was right. "I suppose I can't leave my mother." Her mother would be impossible to take along, and she shouldn't be left alone in this crowd. Even before her accident, Mrs. Bell irritated people with her remarks.

Dinah nodded. "We'll have to wait until tomorrow."

"Tomorrow," Olive said, and dropped back.

Ben shook his head. "Is bad to wait. Bad men. Not police."

Dinah's mouth flew open. If they weren't the police, were they Pinkertons? She raised her eyebrows and mouthed the word. Ben shrugged and disappeared into the crowd.

A well-dressed man on the sidewalk shook his fist and shouted, "Go home for the sake of law and order."

A man jostled through the women to shake his sign. It read: ORDER AND EMPTY STOMACHS CAN NEVER BE ALLIES.

The crowd passed a happier message: "A ball tonight. It's given by the Trades and Labor Assembly." Dinah knew there would be dancing at all the beer halls and saloons that night.

As soon as the line of march stopped, bands all along played the French workers' anthem, *"La Marseillaise."* Dinah sang some of the French words. After the anthem men began speeches, but she didn't listen. I know their speeches by heart, she thought. My job is to free my papa, and how will I do that?

Glancing behind her, she spied some of the seamstresses on the sidewalk, returning to the sewing factory. She followed until she reached Washington Street. When she whistled, a warble answered her; Olive was right behind. They were on their way to the church.

Because fewer immigrants had come for soup that day,

Dinah and Olive each drank two bowls of thick lentil soup, and Dinah stored a dozen rolls in her skirt pockets.

Back at her sewing machine she fed her apple friend, the attendants, and other women with the rolls. The manager wasn't there. Would she lose her job?

But more important, where was her father now?

Her feet rocked the treadle, sewing pockets on shirt fronts, but she was thinking about her papa.

There were footsteps in the back. Without turning, she sensed the manager. Hairs rose on Dinah's neck. All the women slowed their machines.

"Now, girls," shouted the manager, "I told you . . ." Dinah heard a second set of steps. When she glanced behind, she saw the factory owner she had seen with the manager.

"Here you are," the owner said. He and the manager were side by side. To her glance, all but two sewing machines had women sewing. The attendants stood holding shirts. One sank into one of the empty chairs, and the other followed into the second chair. Now all the machines had workers.

As she listened, Dinah bent her head and stitched slower so she could hear clearly.

"So they all stayed at the wheels of industry?"

"Wheels? Uh, yes, sir," said the manager.

"Thirty thousand are on strike for this Eight-Hour Day. They estimated some eighty thousand marched, but your girls are all here. Good for you, Mr. Brown."

"It's Brunsweiger, sir."

"Mr. Brown, increase the girls' day from sixteen to eighteen hours. We'll show them."

"It's Brunsweiger, sir."

"You were born here, weren't you, Mr. Brown?"

"Yes, sir."

"These immigrant girls were meant for labor. They only need time to sleep and return to clean, honest work."

"Yes, sir."

"Clean, honest labor, that's what we provide, Mr. Brown."

"Could we pay them today, sir? It's Saturday, and rents are due on Saturday."

"No, no. Never go back on a promise. You promised them wages on Monday; keep your promise." Dinah saw the owner pat the manager on his shoulder, and she almost laughed. The manager had been about to scold them, or even fire them, but when the owner came, it all changed. Her manager was afraid, too.

He had even tried to pay them. Maybe he cared about them. What would it feel like to be a manager and work for that owner?

"Good-bye, Mr. Brown. I have other factories to visit." The owner lowered his voice. "And I must say, Mr. Brown, you've kept your girls at the wheels of industry better than most. Congratulations!"

So the seamstresses had marched and kept their jobs, too! Dinah felt so relieved she wanted to cry, even while she laughed.

Sunday morning Dinah's mother cooked oatmeal. It seemed strange to have the stove hot in the morning.

While talking to Olive, Dinah heard something. Her heart skipped and she turned around, expecting to see

Olive's dead brother, Josef. Olive gasped—so she had heard, too! A Zagorski boy was bouncing a red rubber ball like Josef's. Dinah closed her eyes. She squeezed Olive's hand, and Olive squeezed back.

When the cereal was cooked, Mrs. Bell fed the family. She had judged the amount for one bowl each. The family ate quietly so the neighbors wouldn't feel left out.

Dinah ate her oatmeal and lay back under the table. No work on Sunday; today she had to find her father. Hands behind her head, she stared out the window until she heard a clatter.

Wild footsteps raced up the wooden stairs then Ben ran in, calling out in German. He jerked Dinah's hand, and Olive took the other hand. Together they pulled Dinah out the door and down the hall. When they were safe in the Peersons' room, Olive turned to Dinah and spit out words in German.

Dinah shook Olive's shoulders. "Speak English, speak English!"

For a while Olive seemed so frightened, she could only remember German. Then she said, "Two men for Bells be coming."

"Two men?"

"For Mr. Noah Bell family asking," said Olive.

Dinah turned toward the door. "Then I better go back."

"*Nein*," Ben whispered, jerking her arm. "Your mother safe, but don't want police to see us." He said something else.

Olive turned to Dinah. "*Achtung!* They with Mr.

77

Meinrad Vonbusch talk. They say you Bells can live in room no longer."

"What? But it's our tenement room."

"For your papa's union work with coloreds," said Ben, "Bells out, without home."

CHAPTER TWELVE

Dinah peeked from the Swedish neighbors' door. Rough-looking men were carrying out her parents' bed, their wardrobe, and all their clothing. Last of all, her screaming mother appeared at the door of their room.

"And I'm a poor disabled woman. And why am I to suffer for my husband's work? In our own family a child starved. This is wrong, wrong, wrong!"

Dinah felt both angry and pleased. Her mother fussed about the immigrants, but she had called Josef "family." Yet, what did her mother's disability, or Josef's death, have to do with being evicted?

Mrs. Mary Bell was lifted between two men and carried out.

"No, no," she called, "Mr. Noah Bell rented that

room. How dare you put us out? We paid the rent Saturday morning. I'll take you to court for this!" Dinah saw her mother shaking a fist.

"Is there no justice in this world? And how dare you do this? Don't you know I have aristocracy in my veins?" Her voice grew fainter as they carried her down the four flights of stairs.

"*Achtung!* Dinah see," Olive said, leaning over the rail.

Dinah glimpsed the Desplaines Street policeman who had helped them. "Why is he doing this?" she asked Olive.

"Why not?" said Ben, shrugging. "They following orders."

Head down, Dinah covered her face. "Orders," Ben had said. Just as the speakers had warned: It was the system, not the people.

When the policemen and hired men had left, Dinah ran down the steps. She and her mother hugged and wept. The Bells had joined the homeless people in the alley.

When her mother stopped sobbing, she told Dinah, "And they told me to take a train out of Chicago. They said we weren't safe here. They said not to wait for Mr. Noah Bell, because I might never see him again." She held Dinah tightly with her one arm.

Not see Papa again? Dinah pushed her crying mother away. "Can you stay here?" she asked. "I have to take Napoleon and find Papa."

Mrs. Bell clutched Dinah's arm. "And how do you

think you'll find him if the police say . . ." Mrs. Bell stopped talking and cried on Dinah's shoulder. "And don't you dare leave your poor helpless mother. What am I to do? No husband, no home. Don't you children ever think about anyone else?"

Olive ran to Dinah's side. "*Jetzt,*" she said. "Now. We must go. To search for your father."

Shaking herself loose from her mother, Dinah said, "Mama, we have to try. Ben saw Papa yesterday."

Her mother's mouth dropped open. "And why didn't you tell me? And who do you think—"

At the end of the alley Ben had been talking to some men; he waved and called, "*Gefahr.*" Olive pulled Dinah and Mrs. Bell into the shadows under the stairs. The two men returned and carried a trunk up to the fourth floor. They escorted a man, and a woman carrying an infant, up the steps.

Bundles followed the new family, and Ben ran off to find out what was going on. Dinah hid under the stairs and held her mother's hand. The men ignored the crowd that had gathered in the alley.

As the men were leaving, Ben returned, sided up to the Bells, and pointed. "That family for telling. Bad for Mr. Vonbusch."

"What does that mean?" asked Dinah. She and her mother huddled by their things near the back door to the saloon. A union man who had been watching leaned out the door.

"It means they've moved in a family to spy on our meetings. Child, could you hear us from your room?"

"Yes, sir," Dinah said. "We heard almost every word, even in the winter."

The man closed the door to the meeting room.

When he opened it again, eight men walked out with him. Mr. Ascher was the last one. He put an arm around Mrs. Bell and patted Dinah's shoulder.

In a low voice he said, "We won't let Mr. Noah Bell's family suffer. Mr. Bell added hundreds of members—colored and white—to the unions. Don't worry. Until you can leave, we'll find you somewhere to stay."

Dinah's eyes opened wide. What did he mean by "until you can leave"? She said, "Yes, sir," politely, but she felt angry and upset.

This was awful. People were talking as if her father would never return. They were treating her mother like a widow, and her like an orphan, but her father was alive. At least he had been yesterday. She had the rosary to prove it.

Today, Sunday, she would find her papa. She must find him. Surely Napoleon could find where they were keeping him?

She piled clothes on top of the wardrobe. All they owned in the world fit into so little space. She could have cried like her mother, but there was too much to do.

Wailing in German, Mrs. Schaffer joined them in the alley.

Mr. Zagorski folded his arms and shook his head; his wife was wringing her hands. The three Schaffer babies stared at Dinah.

"Mama," Dinah said, "the family is here."

"And thank God it isn't cold or raining," her mother

said, looking up. She picked up the ten-gallon pot and handed it to Mrs. Schaffer. "Now she'll feed the family, and we'll starve."

"No, no, Mama," said Dinah.

There were screams from the fourth floor, and union men carried the spy family down the stairs. Their trunk was toppled over the railing, and men walked out of the alley with the family and their belongings.

Mr. Vonbusch beckoned, and Dinah pulled her mother over to listen. "I rent my saloon from the landlord, so I can't keep you here," he told them. "But there's a basement two blocks away. The Ruttenberg children sleep there now. The owner isn't one of us, but he wants someone else to be responsible for the girls." He shrugged. "Besides, they need a woman's care."

He turned to Mrs. Bell. "We could work out a deal. If you'd be willing to take care of the Ruttenberg children, I'll see that you can move in, rent free. But you'll be hiding there. You'll have to come and go in secret."

"Yes, we'll take it," Dinah said quickly, "and thank you."

"What did I do to deserve this?" her mother asked, turning to stare at Dinah. "Colored women been raising white children since the beginning of this country; am I back to slavery days?"

Oh, shut up before he changes his mind, Dinah thought. The man's offered us rent-free shelter.

Her mother went on: "No dignity, and I'm to hide like a rat in a sewer?"

Upstairs, roaches; downstairs, roaches and rats, Dinah thought. But at least they would have shelter.

Within half an hour, union men had carried the Bells' furniture and clothes out of the alley. Olive and Dinah followed with Mrs. Bell. All the way she kept fussing.

"And that my life should come to this, and we have aristocracy in our blood. Where am I now?"

Yes, thought Dinah, where are we now?

CHAPTER THIRTEEN

Standing outside a bakery, Olive, Dinah, and Mrs. Bell listened as Mr. Vonbusch argued with Mr. Kadolph, the owner of the cellar. Sniffing the aroma of baking bread, Dinah felt hopeful. How bad could this be?

She understood some German: the baker hadn't known that they were Negroes, and he thought they looked *wurmstichig*, worm-eaten. When she glanced at her skirt, with its patches and pocket openings, she raised her eyebrows. It was true. She had to change that, but how?

Besides, didn't he see how pretty they were? Everyone remarked about Dinah's pretty face and her mother's beauty. Her father said his "girls" were as pretty as roses in summertime. Dinah touched her braided crown as Mr. Vonbusch argued.

Finally Mr. Kadolph took a huge bunch of keys and pulled one off. Descending an outside stairway, he opened a door to the cellar of his bakery shop and held out the key. Olive, Dinah, and her mother followed him inside to a brick basement.

The Ruttenberg girls, already there, tottered up to them. When Mr. Vonbusch told them something, they hugged Mrs. Bell. For a few seconds she looked shocked; then with her one arm she hugged them back, and Dinah felt a surprising stab of jealousy.

Her mother, who forgot to save soup for her only child, was now going to take care of three other girls! Dinah took a deep breath. Would her mother be responsible enough? Suppose the girls died? They were half starved already and seemed as weak as newborn kittens.

On the other hand, what a good deal this was. Dinah glanced around; the spacious cellar would be warm in winter and cool in summer. Mr. Vonbusch stored kegs of beer there, and the baker kept vats of rising dough. Both the beer and the dough smelled good.

The Bells' things were moved into a back room. Their wardrobe fit into a corner, and her mother put their bed in the center of the space. Moss grew on bricks near the dim light, and the sweating walls glistened. Dinah could tell that her mother didn't want to sleep near damp walls.

Dinah missed her fourth-floor windows to the sky. Standing by a painted window, she used her fingernails to scrape off a flake of paint.

"*Nein*," shouted Mr. Kadolph, waving his arms.

"No, no," Mr. Vonbusch said, "the windows are painted for a reason. Mr. Kadolph and I don't want hungry people knowing we have food and drink stored here. He agrees that you don't have to pay rent; but you must care for the Ruttenberg children and keep the secret of the cellar. Gretchen Ruttenberg was a distant cousin of Mr. Kadolph, but he doesn't want to raise her children."

Why did he let her starve to death? Dinah wondered. He was a selfish man if he made bread but let his cousin, her husband, and some of their children die of hunger!

"I'll care for the children," Mrs. Mary Bell said. She sat on her bed and drew them close.

So, this German cousin let some of a family die, but Dinah's mother would care for the rest. As Olive spoke to the children in German, Dinah took a fresh look at her mother.

For months her mother had shared their tenement room and had cooked for two other families and neighbors; now she was agreeing to care for three children. In spite of her bitterness and fussing, her mother helped people. It was a new look at a mother Dinah thought she knew.

She and Olive raised eyebrows at each other, and Olive began to giggle.

Dinah pointed to Napoleon. "He sleeps inside with us for safety," she said.

"But he our dog is," said Olive.

"Yes, so? He sleeps outside in the alley now."

When Mr. Kadolph understood what Dinah had said,

he smiled and walked over to a flap of stiff leather on the side wall. He raised it and whistled. Trotting over, Napoleon sniffed the fresh air, and Dinah could hear people beside the bakery.

Some bricks had been removed to form a chute that her dog could use to come and go freely. It was too small for a thief of any age, but perfect for a little short-legged dog. This baker was more kind to animals than to people. Dinah wondered what other dog had used the chute.

Looking around, she realized that because people respected her father, she now had somewhere to live, and three little sisters in the bargain. Their living area had a pinewood divider with a door that gave them privacy. And it was warm, with the smell of bread and beer.

As he was leaving, Mr. Vonbusch told them, "Mr. Kadolph's wife and children died of typhoid years ago. He and a cousin run the bakery now."

Time for us to leave, too, Dinah thought. Handing her mother the key, she started up the steps after Olive and the men.

"And Dinah," called her mother, "when you return, I might be out with the children. I heard about a Sunday soup kitchen, and I'll have to tell Mr. Kadolph I must have a stove. And Mr. Vonbusch, you tell . . ."

With Napoleon, Dinah and Olive ran out giggling.

"Here's where Ben said he saw him," said Dinah, pointing. They were near factories and warehouses. Since no one worked on Sunday, workers and their families had come out to stroll and talk.

Olive said. "I am hearing music."

Dinah heard the faint *oompah* of a band. With the other workers they ran to watch a small parade.

After a while Dinah moved away, and Olive followed. Dinah's job was finding her father; she couldn't get distracted. She watched Napoleon carefully—did he sniff anything? Since he didn't seem to be picking up any scents, Dinah held out the rosary from her pocket.

"Here, Napoleon, lead us to Papa." The dog sniffed the rosary. "Where is Papa, Napoleon?"

Napoleon wagged his stump, and Olive petted him.

"The last time, he carried me to the station," said Dinah. "And my father was there."

Napoleon set off slowly, and they followed, strolling along the street. Stores and shops were closed for Sunday. Church bells rang the noon Angelus, and carriages passed carrying families home from church services.

Suddenly Olive, who tailed behind, called, *"Gefahr!"*

Dinah turned quickly when she heard a scuffle. Olive was struggling with a tall man.

Red faced, he was growling like an attack dog. Olive wasted no breath screaming. She wrestled with the man for her life. When Dinah got over the shock, she backed away at first. They had always agreed to run if one of them was caught. But this was different; she couldn't leave Olive—her sister, her friend—with this man. She ran at him and kicked.

Over and over she danced in, kicked his shins, and danced back. He was hurting. Olive got free enough to bite his hand. He tried to hold her and grab for Dinah, but Dinah kept out of reach. Next she began kicking at his knees. She had to free Olive, and with a bad knee the man couldn't chase them.

Another man strolled toward them. "Get these riffraff," the first man shouted. "They stole my money!"

Now Dinah remembered him; he was the Pinkerton detective. The other man began running to his aid. Dinah saw fear in Olive's eyes, but Dinah hadn't been caught. It was up to her to do something.

CHAPTER FOURTEEN

As she fought the man, Dinah called Napoleon. When he ran to her, he stood by her side, wagging his rump. She didn't know what to tell him. Olive had taught him to bark; but Olive was breathless from wrestling the man.

One of Dinah's kicks had injured the man's knee. He was dancing with it bent, but he still held Olive's head in the crook of his elbow, choking her.

"Go, go," called Olive in a hoarse whisper.

The second man was within lunging distance. Dinah swung her shawl over the first man's face. He pulled back, and Olive was free. By then the second man had his hand on Dinah's shoulder, and his fingers dug under her collarbone.

She had to move quickly, before he got his other hand on her. With her back to him, she struck his knee with her heel, turned, and bit his hand. He let go. Free now, she and Olive ran in different directions.

The Pinkerton detective called, "Bobtail thieves!"

"Alley rats," called the other man.

Dinah felt angry; she might be a thief, but she wasn't an alley rat. Besides, she had freed Olive and escaped those men. She was victorious; she had won the battle.

As she ran, she heard band music at another parade. A crowd had gathered; she would hide among them. Dinah was breathless from running, and her heart was pounding. She slid into a group of people and stood beside a tall woman who glanced down at her. "In trouble, honey child?"

Dinah gazed at her brown face, how wonderful. "Chased, ma'am," she said, holding her heart.

"Police?"

Dinah shook her head. "No, ma'am, Pinkertons."

"Worse still." The woman put her arm around Dinah's shoulder. For a second, Dinah felt like crying.

"They may have my father," she told the woman. She felt she could trust this colored lady. It felt good to tell someone.

"Who? The Pinkertons?"

Dinah nodded. "He's a union man. Some men took him from the Twelfth Street jail in a bag."

"In a bag?" said the woman slowly. "Well, there's those who say the Pinkertons have their own jail, and there's those who say that it ain't true. All I know, honey child, is that there's labor men held in an empty factory in the south division."

"Which factory?"

"Would it help you to know? Ain't you got no mama?"

"My mama got her arm cut off."

"Oh, Mrs. Mary Bell, Mrs. Sally's daughter. And your papa be Mr. Noah Bell?"

"Yes, ma'am." Dinah felt like clapping. This lady knew them—her grandmother and her parents. "And I have my dog. He can tell if my papa's in the factory."

"Hound-dog nose." The woman smiled at Napoleon, then she nodded. "We had us a dog like that back home. Couldn't no coon hide from that hound."

She pulled Dinah's chin up. "Well, honey child, there's a factory a whole block long, six blocks south of Madison Street." She explained how to reach it. "Doors be locked, but I been seeing men carried in kicking. Now, don't tell nobody I said so."

"Thank you, ma'am," said Dinah. "Who are you, ma'am?"

"Never you mind. Can I help you more?"

"Yes, ma'am. I threw my shawl over the man's face, and I need one."

"You be wanting mine?"

"Oh yes, ma'am." It was a brown shawl with long fringe.

"And I hope you free your papa. Mr. Noah Bell be a fine colored gentleman."

The large, dressy shawl was long enough to drape over Dinah's head, cover her shoulders, and hang down until she could sit on it. It was a good disguise. "Thank you," she called as she walked away.

The men may not even recognize me now, she

thought. I'll go find that factory while Napoleon's with me. But first I have to find Olive.

Their usual meeting place was at the lakeshore. When Dinah arrived, Sunday speakers were telling crowds about changes in the system, and the Eight-Hour Day. Dinah blended in until she saw the two men searching the crowd. The Pinkerton detective was limping, and his friend was stepping high on one foot. With the dark shawl Dinah covered her head. She bent her shoulders and faked a hobble like an old woman. The men walked right past her.

All along the shore clusters of excited workers gathered. Dinah heard one woman say, "We'll win. Some companies are already discussing a shorter day."

A man said, "Victory is in the air."

"Did you hear?" asked another man. "The lumber shovers are meeting tomorrow afternoon near Black Road."

Meetings, thought Dinah. What good would the meetings do?

Olive was nowhere at the lakeshore. Dinah whistled several times, but Olive's warble didn't answer. Had Olive been hurt? No, she ran too well to have been injured.

Dinah stared at a woman's basket of smoked fish. Since it wasn't for the family, she wouldn't steal. She sighed, pulled out a dry roll, and crunched it. Glancing around, she saw that the Pinkerton detective and his friend had left. Why wait for Olive? Dinah folded the shawl on her arm and trotted to find that factory by herself.

Few people were on the street near the place the

woman had mentioned. That was bad. Looking behind her, Dinah tossed her new shawl over head and shoulders, bent over, and began to hobble. Two unshaven men walked past without a second glance, and she soon found the brick factory that was a city block long.

One end seemed to be for storage—a warehouse—but in the other half of the building, windows had been boarded up. She hobbled at an even pace while Napoleon trotted across the street.

Yes, she saw doors. Four of them, but one door had no dust in the keyhole. It even seemed to have been oiled. Should she call Napoleon, her Blackerton detective dog, to sniff the door? When she looked up, she saw the Pinkerton man again. Was the man they had humbugged holding her father prisoner?

Somehow the idea made her angry. He had called her a bobtail thief, but she stole for a reason. She was almost noble. Of course, he didn't know about that.

Slowly, she hobbled past him. She heard him limp up to the oiled door, open it, and walk in. She hobbled a block farther, then folded her shawl and ran toward home. Napoleon ran on the other side of the street. *I can't wait to tell Olive*, she thought, *but what do I know for sure?*

She longed to find Olive, but first she had to go to the Bells' new home. There, she found too much to do to leave again. Olive and her father would have to wait until Monday.

CHAPTER FIFTEEN

After meeting Olive in the alley Monday morning, Dinah quickly told everything she knew about the empty factory.

"We tonight free your father," said Olive.

"But he's locked in."

Olive pulled a key from her pocket. "*Achtung*. This Pinkerton detective key will opening door."

Dinah had forgotten about the key. She skipped a step. It was settled; after work they would free her father. She felt so happy, she told Olive a joke: "We ran fast yesterday. But do you know who was the fastest runner ever?"

"*Nein*." No.

"Adam. He was first in the human race."

Dinah had to explain because the joke didn't translate

well, but Olive giggled anyway. After walking a few steps, Dinah asked, "How's our money?"

"We having to pay rent next Saturday, so we needing humbug this week. Tomorrow. Next day."

Dinah touched her stomach. Once she had been so weak she thought she might die, but in the cellar that morning she had eaten bread and water for breakfast. That reminded her.

"How was the oatmeal this morning?" she asked.

"Oatmeal was burned black. No one can eating."

"Didn't she cook it over water? You have the two pots."

"My mother fast to cook," Olive said.

Dinah sighed. Her mama was a good cook; that's why the family had left preparing food to her and the girls. There was a lot Dinah hadn't appreciated about her mother.

"I miss the family," said Dinah. "The Ruttenberg girls cry all night. They have bad dreams and keep calling in German."

"Schaffer babies needing you," Olive said, "but I tell them you different blood."

Dinah felt her face grow warm as anger swept over her. Was this Olive talking—her friend, her almost sister? Dinah had thought that the Schaffers were different. They didn't show the prejudices against coloreds that other white people showed. They hadn't been here during slavery in America. Dinah walked backward, facing Olive. "What different blood?"

"What your mama telling."

"What do you mean?" Dinah's voice was icy.

"Something like a-rice-crazy."

"Oh!" Dinah laughed in relief. "You mean when Mama says we have aristocracy in our blood?"

"That. Make you different?"

"No, no, no. It means she had a grandfather who did something grand. I think he tricked the British in Maryland during the War of 1812."

Trickery that was noble, she thought; to save people, he tricked enemy soldiers. Dinah had never thought of it that way before. Desperate measures for desperate times.

"No different in blood, then we can be family."

"Yes, Olive, we're family."

As they left the alley and separated, Olive called softly, "But your grandfather noble, and we humbug thieves." Dinah glanced back at Olive. She hadn't heard her worry about humbug before; at least, she hadn't talked about it.

Later, as they neared the sewing factory, they came together again, and Dinah whispered to Olive, "Maybe what my mother's grandfather did wasn't so different from humbug. He sneaked captive American sailors off a British ship and saved them. We steal money to save our family." She closed her eyes and thought of Josef and the red ball.

As they each turned to go to their separate sewing machines, she whispered, "Soup kitchen at noon."

Olive nodded.

Because Dinah was eager to rescue her papa, the morning seemed longer than usual. All that excitement about the Eight-Hour Day, and they were still working twelve hours; the women worked sixteen. There was that meeting Tuesday night to look forward to, though. Women and girls who sewed might organize into a union.

Individually they could be fired for complaining, but if they complained as a group, they might be heard. Or they might be fired as a group, and other workers hired. Dinah frowned.

At least she could look forward to freeing her father. Would there be guards? How many men had been carried in kicking?

At noon she and Olive ran for a quick lunch. Dinah's soup, bread, and milk gave her energy. When she returned, she shared extra rolls with the two attendants, her apple lady, and others. She knew that all the women were hungry, and as long as she shared, they wouldn't tell on her. Now she only had to sew for the long afternoon.

She was stitching shirt collars, and while she did it, she could daydream. Her thoughts were usually about eating food and wearing pretty dresses. But today she thought only about rescuing her papa. Wouldn't he be proud of her? Would he be surprised to find that their family was now twenty with the Ruttenberg girls? Not seventeen, but twenty to feed.

At midafternoon they heard shouts outside. People were running and calling. But it's been so peaceful, Dinah thought. What could have happened?

A boy ran in. "Mama, Mama," he called. He told his mother something in Polish, and she screamed.

Dinah turned to a Polish lady. "Police are attacking lumber shovers on Black Road," the woman said.

Pointing, she added, "Her husband been badly clubbed by police. Shooting, too."

The manager called, "Girls, back to your sewing. Keep those treadles humming if you want your pay this Monday."

Oh, no, thought Dinah. What had happened to make the police attack? As the afternoon wore on, they learned more. A man crept in and whispered to his wife, then left.

"Black Road is right near McCormick's," the apple lady told Dinah in a whisper. "When new McCormick metalworkers came out, the old metalworkers threw stones at them."

Dinah nodded. That had happened before. This was more to tell her father tonight.

"Keep sewing, girls. Don't cause a ruckus here," said the manager.

A couple of hours later boys shouted in the sewing factory windows: "Many injured. All workers. Two workers killed."

Another man told them, "About six thousand gathered, and five hundred or more went to heckle those new hires. Bulldog Bonfield and two hundred police attacked them. Clubs flying everywhere, then some police opened fire. It was terrible."

Three children ran in, called in Bohemian, and pulled out their mother, screaming and pulling at her hair. Dinah's hands began to tremble. Her feet weren't able to keep the treadle rocking smoothly. On Saturday and Sunday it had seemed that they had a victory; now workers were suffering again.

Those McCormick men, like her father and his friends, wanted their jobs back. Their families were not only hungry, some were starving. And the blacklisted men couldn't work anywhere else. All day she had been happy about freeing her papa, but now she felt angry.

All around her the sniffs and sobs were like a concert of sorrow. At seven, when Dinah and Olive left, they realized that the women had four more hours before they would find out if sons or brothers or husbands had been injured.

Crowds on the streets were all talking. Women stood outside their tenement buildings, waiting for word about some loved one at the meeting.

Dinah and Olive, walking separately, slipped through the crowds, winding their path toward the empty factory where Dinah's father might be. On the way they bought meat and vegetables.

"Ben will meet us," said Olive. "He taking food home. Like from farm in valley, I gather, he carry home."

"Good," Dinah said, leaving her meat with Olive. Over her shoulder she watched Olive pass the bundles to her brother. Now she had to see if she could find her papa in that long building.

CHAPTER SIXTEEN

When they reached quiet streets near the factory, Olive told Dinah, "You watch for Pinkertons. You over there. I with key going." Napoleon lay down near Dinah.

"I'll whistle if there's danger," Dinah called. No one was around. Dinah patted the brown scarf that was tied under her dress. She wore an old tan scarf because working girls wore them, but if she needed to escape, she could use the brown one.

Glancing from side to side, Dinah walked in shadows against the buildings. Across the street from the boarded-up factory she found a narrow alleyway that was around the corner from the oiled door. As she hid there, the factory's boarded windows seemed to stare down at her.

Olive darted to the door. Dinah watched her fumble

the key in the lock, then bend down and stare into the keyhole. Why didn't she open the door?

A wagon turned the corner. It was at the other end of the block, so Dinah didn't whistle. Then the driver gave an order for the horses to trot faster. That could mean danger. Had he seen Olive? Dinah whistled. When Olive turned and waved her hand, Napoleon raced across the street to her. Had Olive forgotten that that was his signal to come?

When he reached Olive's side, Napoleon sniffed the door. Dinah watched. Could her detective dog tell if her father was there? Head down, the dog raced back and forth across the entrance. Then he raised his head and howled.

That meant that Papa was there, but the wagon was closer now. Dinah whistled again. Could Olive hear above the dog's howling? As the man rolled closer, he stood. Dinah watched him, then glanced back at the factory door. Olive had disappeared.

Suddenly, Napoleon stopped howling. He rolled on his back with four feet raised. The driver sat down and chuckled. As he reached the door, he tossed a package out of the wagon. Wrapped in newspapers and tied, it landed on the sidewalk. The man drove away around the corner.

He hadn't seen Dinah in the shadows, and it seemed he hadn't seen Olive, either. Like a ghost, Olive rose from a pile of newspapers beside the factory door. She examined and sniffed the package, then darted across the street to join Dinah.

"Smells like bread," Olive said. "And key not opening door. New lock." She tossed the key on the sidewalk. Dinah picked it up. It was a skeleton key, maybe meant for indoor locks. She dropped it in a pocket.

"Napoleon howled," Dinah said. "That means my father's in there." But the factory was boarded up. Without a key to the door, how could they get in?

"We bring Ben to break open the door."

Dinah sat on a ledge. They were both hidden in the narrow alleyway, but it led nowhere. The back was blocked by a wall.

"I wonder if Papa could hear Napoleon?" she said. "I hope he knows we'll rescue him."

"We will break in," Olive said softly. "*So Gottwill.*" God willing. She took Dinah's hand and squeezed it. At that gesture Dinah began to cry, and Olive hugged her.

After a while Olive shook Dinah's shoulder. "*Gefahr!*" Glancing up, Dinah saw a man turn the corner, pick up the package, and stride up to the factory. Opening the door with a key, he walked in, carrying the bundle.

"Your papa will eat," Olive said.

Dinah picked up Napoleon. "Suppose we send him in?"

"Why?"

"To find my papa."

The door slammed shut.

"Now too late."

The girls crouched in the dark alleyway.

On the next street Dinah heard men calling. Others shouted back at them, but it was all in German and

Bohemian. Olive squeezed her shoulder. "*Achtung!* Meeting for protest will be."

"When?" asked Dinah.

"Tomorrow. Tuesday, May fourth. Seven thirty."

"Maybe if we hurry, we can make it after work." Dinah wanted to go to the seamstress' meeting, too, but maybe this was more important. "Where will it be?" she asked Olive.

"Haymarket Square."

Oh, thought Dinah, Haymarket Square. They're expecting a crowd, then. I bet workers are angry about the police shooting them at McCormick's this morning.

"Maybe," she said, "just maybe, my papa can go, too." She glanced behind her at the darkness in that alley. Olive always said not to hide in a place with one entrance. But this was across the street from the boarded-up factory.

The man opened the door again. "Get Papa," ordered Dinah, and she pushed Napoleon toward the factory door.

The dog raced across the street, barking all the way. The man turned around in the doorway. Bumping him, Napoleon ran between his legs and began to howl. The man ran inside after the dog and left the door open.

Olive and Dinah glanced at each other. Olive shook her head no, but Dinah said, "Yes." She raced toward that open door. She heard Olive shout, "*Gefahr!*" For her to call aloud, the danger must be great, perhaps people coming, but it was too late to turn back. Dinah ran through the door and down a dark hall.

On every side doors were shut. She ran up and shook

one, then another and another. They were locked. Soon she had run so far the light from the open door was gone. Panting, she slowed to a walk.

The factory had large rooms on either side of a central hall. Dirty skylights in the high ceiling let in the dim light of evening. When she stopped, she heard nothing. Not Napoleon, not the man. She turned around.

In the distant doorway, the one she had entered, she saw silhouettes of two men who stood staring in. So that's why Olive had shouted a warning. Should she whistle for Napoleon? Where was that first man? Did he know that she was inside?

Dinah's heart pounded as she crouched low. Three men now.

Alone, she could not rescue her father from three men. The man who carried the bread might know she was in there, or he might not know. The other two men had probably seen her. She had to get out and return with Ben. Finally she heard footsteps.

Backing into a dark doorway, she stood leaning within it, hoping to look part of the shadow. The man was coming, and he would pass her. He was carrying something; of course, he carried Napoleon. Her dog whined. She extended her arms to hug the door behind her. Be good, Napoleon, she thought. Don't let the man know that I'm here.

"What is it?" called one of the men in the entrance doorway.

"Must be a union worker's dog," answered the first man. "Raced right to their vault. I got him, though."

"I meant to tell you," said one man, "we heard from a

spy that a little colored girl might try to break in."

The other men laughed. "A little girl?"

Dinah felt hairs rise on her arms. What spy?

"Says the raggedy child will be wearing a brown scarf. She knows because she gave the scarf to the child."

"You paid her for that?"

"Sure. Five cents for bread," he said. "This colored woman visits all the saloons, takes part in marches, carries water to men on strike. We've gotten good information from her."

A spy, Dinah thought, a colored spy. How awful. She felt her face grow hot. If the woman was a spy, had the woman lied to her? Was her father even in here? Well, it was the only place she knew to try. What should she do now?

If she stayed inside, she could try that skeleton key on the doors in the hall. Olive would tell Ben where she was. Locked in by herself she might find her papa. If he was there.

"Well," one man said, "a child would need an army to break into this building. I think the woman's a liar."

The man reached the door with Napoleon. Dinah heard Napoleon hit the street with a thud and a yelp. Wincing, she clutched the wall. Did the dog break any bones?

"Want me to shoot him?" one man asked, fumbling with his side.

Dinah's heart raced. The three men were silhouetted by gaslight from the streets. She wanted to run and grab that gun. She couldn't let that man shoot her dog.

"Listen," the third man said. "Hear them calling?

There's going to be a protest meeting tomorrow. Haymarket Square. We'll see plenty of action then."

He laughed and added, "Yes, shoot the dog. We don't want any anarchist's dog giving this place away."

Dinah could hardly breathe and her heart was drumming, but she had to save Napoleon. The man was taking his gun out of a hip holster. The time was now or never. She took a deep breath. Three men. Talking. A door slowly closing. They weren't expecting her. It would be a surprise. Get there before that door closed.

Arms pumping, she raced for the door. Running, running down the long hall. She flung the door open and pushed the two men aside. The door struck the third man. She heard his gun fall and skid on the sidewalk. It didn't go off. Past the three men she ran. Napoleon was safe; she heard him panting beside her.

She raced for the alleyway. She knew she shouldn't, but she heard the thudding footsteps of the men who were chasing her, and she couldn't think straight. She was giving Olive away. They would both be trapped in a dead-end alley.

CHAPTER SEVENTEEN

The alley was so narrow the men behind her had to run in single file, bumping the walls. Olive led Dinah running. But where? Dinah saw a wall of darkness, and Olive whispered something in German. Why couldn't she say it in English? What was Olive trying to tell her?

She heard Olive hit that wall. She seemed to be scratching at the bricks. Climbing. She was climbing up. Dinah heard her panting above her, heard her jump down and keep running.

When Dinah hit the wall, it hurt her chin and ribs. She used her hands, tried to pull herself up. She fell back. Again she tried, scrambling with hands and feet. The men were gaining on her. She jumped and tried her feet against the bricks; Olive had done it. She fell back.

I can't get over the wall like Olive, she thought in

terror. The sound of the men's thudding footsteps grew closer. What should she do? Bending low, she curled up at the bottom of the wall. Pulling out that dark scarf, she covered herself and pulled her skirts in, then held her breath. Her heart sounded so loud, she was sure its pounding would give her away.

Before they reached her, the men stopped.

"She's gone," one man said.

"Over some kind of wall. A crossway meets the alley here. She's gone."

"What happened to the dog?" another man asked.

"I hear him panting."

Yes, Dinah heard him, too. Slowly she reached her hand and touched his fur. She left her hand there. Napoleon sat still.

"I could shoot him here."

"Maybe you should."

Dinah kept her hand on her dog.

"Wait. Maybe not. A shot might alert curious people. I say we forget this whole affair. A little girl like that getting into the building could make us look like fools."

"And," said the first man, "I left the door open. Better get back there." They turned and walked single file out of the alleyway.

Dinah's heart eased its pounding; she patted Napoleon. When the men reached the street, Dinah saw their shadows against the boarded-up factory where her father might be a prisoner.

The next day, Tuesday, Dinah was surprised that people didn't seem eager to go to the protest meeting at

Haymarket Square. At noon she and Olive slipped into the soup kitchen and heard Father O'Connor say, "Not me. I'm not for setting the good monsignor sputtering again like a wick out of wax."

"The people must feel so disappointed," said Miss Hallelujah.

Dinah and Olive were silent as they ate. On the way back to their sewing factory, Dinah said, "Even if no one else is going, I'm going."

"But," said Olive, "we tonight rescue your father."

"I don't know," Dinah said, "maybe we should free him Wednesday. They'll be looking for us tonight."

Olive nodded. "I will check on men. You go to protest. I buy all food. Your mama comes to cook again, we eating good."

Dinah nodded. Olive would buy both the meat and the vegetables. Monday night Dinah's mother had returned to the fourth floor to cook for everyone, including her new daughters. After they ate, Mrs. Bell walked her three little girls back to sneak into the cellar of Kadolph's Bakery.

After work that evening, Tuesday, May 4, Dinah felt free. Going to Haymarket Square would be like taking her father's place, and she could tell him about the protest. She arrived at seven thirty by church bells.

When she found that the square was almost empty, she felt angry. How dare they forget so soon? Men had been clubbed and killed, and this was only the day after. Where was everyone?

Soon families began to appear—strolling parents, skipping children. Dinah estimated about twenty-five hundred finally gathered. Streetcars ran down Randolph Street, and riders on the streetcars stared at them.

A man in the crowd said, "This meeting was poorly planned."

"They got the proper permits," another man said. "The police can't bother us here. Besides, isn't that Mayor Harrison riding over there?"

Dinah glanced quickly. Mayor Carter Harrison was dressed in a coat with no tie, and he rode a white horse.

Church bells rang eight thirty; an hour had passed, and no speakers had arrived yet. Finally Mr. August Spies ran up.

He walked around in the crowd, asking questions. When Dinah went up to him, she couldn't understand his German, but she could read what a man held out to him. It was a handbill printed in both German and English. She read the English:

Attention workingmen!
Great
mass-meeting
to-night, at 7:30 o'clock,
at the
Haymarket, Randolph St.,
Bet. Desplaines and Halsted.
Good speakers will be present
to denounce the latest
atrocious act of the police, the shooting of
our fellow-workmen yesterday afternoon.
The Executive Committee.

❖ ❖ ❖

After glancing around, Mr. Spies rolled an abandoned wagon free. He pulled it over to an alleyway between Crane's Factory and another factory on Desplaines Street.

"We won't block the streetcars," he said. "We don't have enough workers here for that." Now they were no longer in Haymarket Square, but at Crane's Alley. With her back to the wagon, Dinah looked two blocks south to the Desplaines Street police station, where she had searched for her father.

Dinah pulled a roll from her pocket for dinner. She hid the roll in her fist and ate it slowly. Around her people stared at her bread.

She watched Mr. Spies climb up on the wagon to speak. But before he said anything, he called to a man. "Can you find Mr. Parsons? See if Mr. Fielden's around, too. They have to come and speak."

Finally Mr. Spies began talking about the reason for the meeting. The people listened as if they were starved for words of hope. Of course, Dinah thought, we're all discouraged. She left the front of the crowd and wove a path to the back.

She was glad she did, because at the back she saw Mr. and Mrs. Parsons arrive. Mrs. Lucy Parsons carried Lulu, and Mr. Albert Parsons had Albert Jr. by the hand. Mr. Parsons smiled and nodded at Dinah. His black hair and mustache were neatly trimmed as usual.

He put his wife and children, along with Mrs. Lizzie Holmes, on a wagon north of the speaker's wagon. Dinah guessed the seamstresses' meeting hadn't lasted long, since Mrs. Parsons and Mrs. Holmes were here.

When Mr. Parsons climbed up on the wagon, he

spoke for almost an hour. Dinah liked the way he talked. His tenor voice was musical, and she believed what he said. But she was tired; she yawned. Could she last this whole meeting? After Mr. Parsons, Mr. Samuel Fielden jumped up on the wagon. Next to Mr. Parsons, Mr. Fielden, with his bushy black eyebrows, was her favorite speaker. He spoke in a British accent and often quoted the Bible. His wife and two-year-old daughter were there.

Regardless of which language the speakers spoke, there were restless immigrant workers who couldn't understand. To stay awake, Dinah walked up and down among them.

A cold wind began to whip dust and straw off the market square behind her. Women gathered their children, and families began to leave. When it started to drizzle, Dinah decided to go home, too.

Church bells rang ten thirty, and she heard shuffling feet. When Dinah glanced behind her, she saw policemen gathering at the Desplaines Street station. They were running into an alley beside the station. She glimpsed Captain John Bonfield, with his square jaw and bushy mustache, and Captain Ward, too.

What is happening? she wondered as she stood and stared. Her scalp tingled. Should she run? But she wanted to know what would happen. She already had something to tell her papa, but maybe there would be more.

At an order, the police marched out of the alley and formed rows from one side of the street to the other. Within minutes they had marched up to the back of the crowd, about two hundred people—only a part of the original group. She estimated that there were about two hundred police, too. Why all these police, she wondered. Are we workers criminals?

Captain Bonfield shouted: "In the name of the people of the State of Illinois, I command this meeting immediately and peaceably to disperse." He glared at Mr. Fielden.

Glancing around, Dinah saw that Mr. Parsons had left with his family and friends. She wanted to leave, too, but now she was hemmed in between the police and the crowd.

Mr. Fielden answered, "But, Captain, we are peaceable." Dinah agreed and nodded. Mr. Fielden stooped to jump down.

From the corner of her eye she saw a tall person in the factory doorway by the alley raise his arm. She saw light; a fuse had been lit to sputter. In the dark she saw a ball with fire behind it thrown into the crowd. The explosion was like a thunderclap. For seconds she was deaf. Police behind her yelled, shuffled, and began to fire their guns.

A worker called, "That was dynamite!"

Arms wrapped around her head, Dinah dropped to the ground.

CHAPTER EIGHTEEN

In the dark that Tuesday night, screaming people panicked, running to and fro. Dinah heard police clubs striking skulls and shoulders. People were moaning. She heard a woman whisper, "They're bleeding."

By gaslight Dinah saw a woman grab her grown son, who had fallen, and drag him through the crowd. Hugging her skirt to her stomach, Dinah began crawling to escape the clubs. While some police were slugging people, others were shooting. Dinah's hand slid in blood, and she wiped it on the pants of a man who stood over her.

Mr. Fielden passed her; he was bleeding.

It seemed to take forever to escape the scuffling. Finally Dinah found herself at the edge of the confusion.

As soon as she cleared the crowd, she stood and ran. Her legs seemed heavy, and she wondered if she could run the many blocks to her alley.

She was so confused, she had passed the usual sleeping immigrants and started up the tenement steps before she remembered that she didn't live there anymore. As she stumbled down, Mr. Vonbusch caught her arm.

"What happened?"

"At the Haymarket meeting," she said in gasps, "the police marched to break it up. A man threw dynamite. Big explosion. Police shooting. Hitting people with clubs. It's terrible." She bent over. Her side hurt from running, and she still heard in her mind the screams and cries of injured people.

Mr. Vonbusch nodded. He disappeared into his back room. Inside Dinah heard men asking, "Did you find out?"

She didn't wait to hear his answer, but ran to her new home. When she tiptoed into the cellar, she smelled food. Not only was her bowl of soup still warm, but she had two chicken wings to suck meat off of, and a warm biscuit. Hands trembling, she ate it all. Then, in exhaustion, she rolled onto her bed with her clothes still on.

Wednesday the city was in an uproar over the bomb. Newspaper boys called, "Read all about it! Now it is blood!" From the sewing factory windows, Dinah saw police wagons rolling past with men and women standing on them.

Why are all those people going to jail? she wondered. Only one man threw the bomb, but who was he? Had the police hired him to give them an excuse to crack down on unions? Or was he an angry worker? And could this keep her from rescuing Papa?

On her job that day two women fainted. A man shouted in the factory windows, "A police dragnet. They're arresting strikers and union people."

His wife called, "Run and hide."

Olive passed Dinah leaving for the soup kitchen. She bumped her. "*Jetzt*," she said softly. Now. They had to free Dinah's father, and fast, that night for sure. They walked to the kitchen separately, but as they sipped their soup, they whispered.

Father O'Connor leaned down. "I'll pray that you are able to rescue your father. I only wish that I had some influence, but in these matters I have none. Police are angry at workers. Officer Degan has been anointed for death. Several policemen may die from wounds. Sad times." He patted their shoulders.

Dinah remembered Officer Degan—he had been at the Desplaines Street desk—and she felt sorry for him. But how many workers had been killed?

That evening she and Olive quickly took supplies for dinner to the fourth-floor room. As the two left with Ben, they came to hungry immigrants sitting on the stairs.

"No meat today," Dinah told them, "but good vegetables." She hoped those who spoke English would tell the others. Olive was saving money for the next rent, but that meant their food money was giving out. They needed humbug.

No, there had to be a better way. She wanted to be a noble person, not a child criminal.

"Olive, Ben," said Dinah as they walked down the steps, "I can't keep up humbug." Yet, what would they do? The family must not starve.

Ben turned quickly. "If police arrest me, I go to jail. I hate humbug." He spoke so violently, Dinah stared at him. No wonder he always seemed angry when they stole.

Olive turned to them both. "We have twenty people in family to feed, and all others we can. But we think of better way. I maybe have plan."

Dinah said, "I hope you do. We have to think of something. I don't want trouble with police or Pinkertons, either. It's awful looking over my shoulder all the time."

At the bottom of the stairs, Olive dragged Dinah aside. "We will be thinking, but come. Ben and me plan yesterday for your papa's rescue. We do good ideas." They walked into Mr. Vonbusch's back room, where a lady from their alley stood by a wooden trunk. On top were two dresses and bonnets. The lady who stood by the trunk kept nodding and smiling.

Olive held up a dress. "She maken shorter for you."

"Oh," Dinah said, looking at the pretty dresses, "we'll look like ladies." Her throat felt tight and her eyes grew wet. She'd look like a lady, but she was a thief.

"Wear over dress. You need pockets," said Olive. Her dress was dark blue, and her bonnet black. Dinah's dress was dark green with a bonnet to match. The dresses had been hemmed to fit them. Ben walked from the saloon dressed in a fine black jacket and derby. When Napoleon sniffed their clothes, he whined, but Olive talked to him in German until he wagged his rump.

They were about to leave when they heard police shouting in the front of the saloon. Ben strolled with them to the back door, where more police met them. One officer had a club in one hand and a gun in the other.

"We're breaking up this union meeting," he called.

What union meeting? Dinah glanced around. The immigrant lady looked terrified. Dinah walked back and squeezed hands with the lady. She and Olive then walked out on Ben's arms. The policeman pushed them aside but didn't stop them. In the alley stood a horse-drawn police wagon. Dinah wondered why Ben smiled.

Arm in arm, strolling slowly, they finally arrived at the block where the boarded-up factory squatted blind and silent. A police wagon passed on a side street, with people riding to a station. Dinah trembled.

All day policemen had been raiding beer halls, saloons, and tenements where striking workers lived. They broke up any gatherings. She knew this made rescuing her father more difficult. What would the police do if they were caught?

Ben glanced at the building. "Window best for free your papa," he told Dinah. He handed her a knife, and she slipped it in her skirt pocket. But what for? she wondered.

When both side streets were bare, Ben pulled an ax and rope from his jacket. He tied the rope on the ax and pushed the girls aside. Swinging the ax around his head, he struck the board over the window. Dinah heard the wood crunch. The ax fell to the street with a metallic thud.

Again Ben swung the ax. This time it stuck in the board briefly, then fell to the street.

Olive whispered, *"Gefahr!"* A carriage was passing.

Ben turned and put his arm around Olive on one side, Dinah on the other. As they stood close, Dinah asked in a whisper, "Do you know what you're doing, Ben Schaffer?"

"Dirty inside?" Ben asked, not answering her.

She nodded.

"Taken dress off," he said. "I open window soon."

Nodding her head, she began unbuttoning.

At the next toss, the ax stuck in the wood boarding the window, and Ben used the rope to climb up. With the claw end of a hammer, he pulled nails from one side of the board. The wood swung out. After nails from the other side came out, Ben jumped to the street with the board falling on top of him. The girls lifted the board and helped him up.

"Good," he said. "Window, no glass." He glanced around.

"Jetzt," he whispered. No one was on the street.

Olive caught Dinah's green dress and pulled it off. She helped Dinah climb onto Ben's shoulders as he stooped. Then slowly he raised her. With both hands Dinah reached up and grabbed the windowsill, hoisted herself, and hung on her stomach. Kicking in the air, she worked one leg over the wide sill until she could lie there. When she glanced back, the board was lying neatly on the sidewalk, and Olive and Ben were gone.

The street was clear, the sidewalk empty. Dinah knew Ben and Olive were only hiding, but she felt terribly alone. She began to tremble so violently that her teeth chattered. Ben and Olive and she were only children. Should they do this, or give up?

She stared down into the dark factory. A mouse scampered by with a squeak. How far was the floor? She had to get down someway, but would she get hurt? Could she break a leg? Taking a deep breath, she jumped down and landed with both knees bent.

Not too far for a jump, but she'd need a ladder to get back up to that windowsill. And she didn't have a ladder. How would she get out? For a moment she felt a wave of panic, but she fought it.

Dirty skylights allowed her to see. She ran to the door of the room and shook the knob. Of course, the doors had been locked when she had tried them from the hall. Would the skeleton key work in here? Her trembling slowed. As she dug in her pockets for the key, she listened.

Everything was quiet. All she could hear was the sound of her heart and the scampering of mice. This must have been a furniture factory, because it smelled of wood.

As soon as she found the skeleton key, she stuck it into the door latch. It fit. Turning the key, she opened the door. Leaving it open, she ran down the hall, remembering that the man had returned from far into the building.

If only she had Napoleon to sniff and tell her where her father was. Would the room have another lock? This was a huge empty factory. Where was her papa?

CHAPTER NINETEEN

More dirty skylights in the roof lent twilight to the hall. Was there a guard? If so, he was silent. Dinah ran banging on doors, but no one called out.

If today was like that other time, in about half an hour a man in a wagon might deliver bread, and another man might come to open the outside door. Dinah hoped they wouldn't be early. She had little enough time to find her father.

All the rooms echoed, hollow, empty. At the end of the long hall she found a metal cage. The grating clanged as she shook what seemed to be a door. She pushed at it with her hands and shoulder. The door groaned open sideways on rusty hinges. She left it open and tiptoed in. What a smell!

"Anybody there?" she called.

She heard a groan. Someone was there. The sharp odors of urine and bowel movements struck her face. Inside the caged room there was another metal door. Dinah pulled and pulled. The door was heavy, but unlocked. When she opened it, the odors from within made her stagger. Her poor papa, was he here? The room was totally dark.

"Are you here?" she asked.

There was a rustling. More than one person was breathing.

"Dinah." The voice was muffled, but she knew it. If only she had light. Wait, that first night. She had taken the candle and matches off the stove. Were they still in her pocket? Yes.

With trembling hands, she lit the candle.

How awful. Seven men sat in a row of chairs. Their mouths were stuffed with gags, their arms and legs tied to the chairs. First Dinah decided to untie the gags. She began with the nearest man; she had to hurry.

Where was her papa? The men all looked alike. She had almost finished untying her father's gag before she realized who he was. Like the other men, his hair and face were white with plaster dust from the ceiling.

"Papa!" She kissed his forehead.

She hurried to remove the rest of the gags. Finishing all seven, she stared at the ropes that tied the men to the chairs.

By candlelight she could see that the men's arms and legs were dark and bloody, as well as swollen. The ropes had cut into their flesh.

How to free them? Ben's knife—he must have known

she would need it. Dinah took a deep breath and almost gagged. Sawing the blade back and forth, she cut, first her father's ropes, then the ropes of all the other men.

Her father tried to rise, and fell to the floor, rolling around. He had trouble straightening his knees and elbows. She pulled him. "Stand up, Papa," she said, "we have to hurry."

He shook his head. "I can't," he said in a hoarse voice. Now all the men were rolling on the floor. They had been tied so long, they couldn't move well. This was a problem she hadn't foreseen. She couldn't walk them out. She couldn't carry them. What could she do now?

Dinah blew out the candle. At least when the bread man came to feed them, he wouldn't know anything until he reached them. She raced back down the long hall, ran in the open door, and stood staring at that impossible windowsill above her. She could never reach it.

But she heard a warble. She whistled back. "I found them," she called. She felt frantic.

"Coming out?" Olive asked.

"No. They're too weak. They can't even stand. I cut them free, but they can't move." Suddenly Dinah felt like crying. So close, and yet she might not be able to save Papa after all.

"And I can't reach this windowsill," she called. "It's too far up."

Olive called, *"Unglaublich."* Dinah watched as a couple of wooden poles rose up, then tottered on the sill. She moved aside. A ladder dropped into the room, and fell. Where had they found the ladder?

It was heavy to lift, almost too heavy. Feeling a surge

of strength, Dinah lifted it and pushed it up against the windowsill. She couldn't leave and she couldn't stay. Even if Ben came in, what good would that do? Climbing up, she looked outside.

When she peeked over the sill, she saw a lady in a bonnet and a gentleman standing by her. For a second, even Dinah was fooled.

"How are they?" Ben asked without looking up.

"They're on the floor, can't stand or walk. I can't get them to this room."

She watched as Ben strolled across the street. He whistled, and workmen in overalls and work pants ran out of the alleyway. One after another they stood on shoulders and dropped into the room. The first man in was Mr. Schaffer. Mr. Zagorski and the fourth-floor Swedish workers followed.

Dinah led them running down the hall. Now she felt powerful. She had an army of workers, and her food had made them strong. Again she lit the candle, but when she turned, she saw the men hadn't followed her into the vault.

Candle in hand, she returned to the door and found two men gagging. Another had his hand across his face. Yes, the odor was bad.

"Hurry," she said.

They walked into the inner room and stood staring. Dinah knelt by her papa and looked back at the workmen. What was wrong with these grown men? Couldn't they do something to help?

She glanced back at her father's mouth. If only she had water to give him. A water bucket and dipper stood by the door, but her papa's tongue seemed swollen from thirst.

Finally the neighbors, who had seemed horrified at first, began to move.

Dinah made sure her father was the first to be picked up. In pairs the men lifted the prisoners, and with crossed hands carried them basket-style down the long hall to the open room. More union workers ran down to join them. One man shouted. The man he had lifted was his brother. They both wept.

"Hurry," Dinah repeated. At last they were moving, but that bread man would be there any moment now.

When all the prisoners were by the window, they tried to lift them, but the prisoners couldn't help themselves at all. They couldn't walk up the ladder. Finally Mr. Schaffer carried Papa over his shoulder up the ladder. Dinah listened. It seemed that men outside caught him as he was dropped. One by one Mr. Schaffer carried the poor men.

Dinah paced the floor. Time was passing. It seemed to take forever to get those prisoners over the sill. Four more were left when she heard Napoleon barking at the outside door. The bread man must have come to feed them, and he was cursing the dog. She blew out her candle.

Inside the room, they continued to push each prisoner over the windowsill and drop him. Dinah felt frantic. Apparently the bread man hadn't noticed the rescue around the corner. Olive must have sent Napoleon to bark at him. Dinah had no idea how the prisoners could be carried away safely after they were freed. That was a problem the people outside would have to solve. She had an even bigger problem inside.

How could she stop the bread man from entering? From finding the prisoners gone?

She tiptoed out of the room. The door was at the end of the hall. Napoleon's barking was frantic. Good dog! Feeling in her pocket, she touched that key. It hadn't been a key to open the outside lock, but could it jam the lock from the inside? It might work. She raced down the hall.

At the door her hands were trembling. She hadn't gotten this far in saving her father only to have him put back in jail. And those other six men. Their wives and children were worried, too.

Napoleon growled. It sounded as if he was tugging at the man's pants. She heard a tearing sound. Then the dog yelped. Had the man kicked him?

First Dinah took soft, hot wax from the candle and tried to plug the lock. Napoleon wasn't bothering the man anymore. She could feel the man's key turning. Pushing the door, she stuck her key in to hold the lock still. It fit against the man's key. She heard him curse. The wax began to harden, keeping her key stuck solid in the lock. It would stay there. Outside, Napoleon kept up his barking, but he sounded farther away.

When Dinah knew the man could not get in, she ran back. The room was empty, but the ladder was still there. She closed the door, ran to the window. Pulling her skirt around her, she climbed up and perched on the windowsill.

Below her about seventeen men huddled silently in shadows by the brick building. At the end of the block a police wagon's horses were trotting rapidly toward them. Oh, no. What could they do? Should she stay in the building? No. She'd go to her father. She closed her eyes and jumped.

CHAPTER TWENTY

When Dinah jumped from the window, Mr. Schaffer caught her. Turning immediately, she found her papa slumped in a Swedish neighbor's arms, and she hugged him quietly. He rested his head on her shoulder. With swollen fingers and clumsy hands, he stroked her face. Now what? she wondered.

Behind her Dinah heard that police wagon rolling, the horses' feet clattering. The crowd of men had frozen. Dinah could hear them breathing in and out as the wagon rolled up to them. Across the street Olive stepped out of the alley. Why? She had been safe.

Olive whispered, "*Jetzt.*"

Dinah stared. Dressed in a police officer's uniform, Ben stopped the horses and leaped down. The jacket hung off his shoulders and the pants were rolled up, but that didn't matter. He passed as a policeman. Dinah almost fainted; they were safe after all.

In no time the seven prisoners and their family of rescuers were standing in the open wagon and rolling away. They looked no different from the police wagons of workmen she had seen all day.

Dinah ran into the alleyway to put on her green dress and bonnet. With the help of neighbors, she had saved her father. Olive sat on a ledge and watched her.

"Thank you," Dinah whispered.

"We am family," said Olive.

After they watched the bread man walk away shaking his head, Dinah signaled for Napoleon to go. Arm in arm Dinah and Olive strolled, with their dog trotting across the street. Dinah still couldn't believe it. They had actually freed her father.

"Hurry," she whispered. "I want to talk to Papa when he gets home."

"No," said Olive, pulling her back. "Ladies not hurry. Besides, Ben will take others home first. Dinah," she added, "I need to talk to you. You leader of humbug. But I think anarchy way to feed family, too."

"Anarchy!" Dinah groaned. "How can anarchy help us? It would take years for an anarchist nongovernment to be set up. And then, according to Papa, it wouldn't work."

"Anarchists call for exchange of work and products. Today buying for family, I talk to butcher, I talk to grocer. They will take work from us. In exchange."

"What?" Dinah's mouth dropped open. What had Olive said?

"*Achtung!* You sweep bloody straw from butcher's shop each evening. You both colored, he give meat to you."

"Oh," Dinah said, raising her eyebrows. Enough to feed the family? The butcher agreed to that?

"Ben and me open crates for grocer. We all Austrian, he give vegetables to us."

Dinah swirled and hugged Olive. "That's wonderful. How wonderful! We can still feed the family, but we don't have to do humbug!" What good news. She felt like yelling for happiness, but, of course, ladies didn't yell.

Across the street Napoleon trotted sniffing the air.

When they arrived at their alley, Dinah saw men scrubbing her bare father at the pump. She reached under her green dress and into her pocket. The bar of soap would help clean his hair and skin. She tossed it to Mr. Schaffer.

After bathing him, the men dumped buckets of rinse water on him and wrapped him in a blanket. Dinah smelled her father's foul clothes burning.

All the way to their new home Mr. Schaffer and Mr. Zagorski carried Papa, wrapped in a blanket, with his arms over their shoulders. With one arm her weeping mother helped him dress, and he was propped up on his bed. The men left, but Ben and Olive stayed. Dinah's father looked around.

"My Mr. Noah Bell is home. Who would have thought he was alive, and now I have my husband home." As tears flowed on her cheeks, Dinah's mother knelt by her husband, stroking his head. "And I love him so much, and I love him all the time, my husband."

Stop it, thought Dinah. You don't love him any more

than I do. He's only your husband, but he's my father. She hesitated, and thought: And you're my mother. My crazy but good-hearted mother. I can accept you, I can love you.

She sniffed. Her mother even smelled good. Of course, she had washed the three little girls and herself. Her mother's arm nub had healed at last, too. She no longer needed to cover it.

If her mother could bathe—even if it was only a bucket bath—Dinah could bathe, too. There was privacy in the bakery basement. Olive could come there and take a bucket bath, too.

No more humbug, either. Thank you, God, Dinah thought.

For a moment Dinah felt that her heart would burst; surely this was a moment when goodness grew out of truth and flowered in beauty. She loved both her mother and her father, and her father was home.

"And Mr. Bell," said her mother, "these little girls of the Ruttenbergs are now our children, too. Since Gretchen and Otto are both dead, we're the only parents they have."

Dinah winced when her mother went on to say, "We're raising white children, like in black slavery days."

When Papa smiled and beckoned to the girls, they grinned and came over. Dinah thought that after only four days, color had risen in their cheeks, and they were stronger. Her mother was feeding them well, and they seemed happier, too.

"Good," Papa whispered in a hoarse voice. "Lo and behold, as part of God's creation, we are all one family of people: colored and white, immigrant and citizen, rich and poor. Together we struggle for a better life."

To Dinah, his talk sounded like a speech. He was always planning for a better life for poor people, but it was going to be worse after that dynamite at Haymarket Square. She shook her head. What a dreamer her father was! But it was wonderful to have him home.

She lifted a cup of soup to his lips. Every few minutes he took a small sip. He couldn't manage to drink much at a time, but already he seemed less stiff.

She described the Saturday march for the Eight-Hour Day in glowing words. When she finished, she took a deep breath. The poor had had power; her father had been right.

"Papa," she said, "it was beautiful." More and more she understood what her father meant by "beautiful."

It needn't be a pretty kind of beauty for the eyes; it was a righteous kind of beauty for the mind. The kind that went with power, glory, truth, and goodness. A beauty that made people's hearts sing. She smiled.

There was a knock on the door. Two union men and Mr. Kadolph stood at the bottom of the stone steps. "Mr. Bell," said Mr. Ascher, "workers have heard your name mentioned tonight. Apparently some policeman thinks you're a sorcerer or some sort of magic person."

"Yes," the other man said. "Workers took out the ladder and nailed the board back over the factory window. When that was done, people had no idea how you and the others escaped."

Dinah glanced across at Olive and Ben; they all

grinned. Dinah still had to find out how Ben had borrowed that police wagon.

"But," said Mr. Ascher, "we think you have to leave Chicago for a few months, until this Haymarket tragedy blows over. They're weaving the legal ropes for hanging. Mr. Albert Parsons has escaped, but they're holding other union leaders."

"They're calling them co-conspirators," said Mr. Ascher.

She knew she shouldn't, but Dinah broke in. "Sir, who threw that dynamite last night?"

"No one knows who threw the dynamite." Both men agreed.

Mr. Kadolph said, *"Gefahr!"*

"Yes, it's dangerous for you to be here," Mr. Ascher told Dinah's father. "We have coloreds in Ohio who need an organizer of their own skin color. More than sixty thousand colored workers are now in the Knights of Labor. We need you there. Officer Mathias J. Degan is bleeding to death, and other policemen are badly wounded. Of course, the workers who were killed or injured didn't make the newspapers."

"Now the police have a 'law and order' cause as a base to their fight with us," the other man said. "One of their own is dying."

Dinah's father struggled to sit forward, and fell back. She gave him another sip of soup.

"We'll carry you," Mr. Ascher said. "There's a midnight train to Ohio. We'll send a coded telegraph message. Workers will meet you there and help you recover."

"If you stay here, you'll be another suspect of the dynamite crime," said the other man.

"He was locked in a cage," shouted Dinah. How could they think he did it? But, on the other hand, if they thought he was a sorcerer?

"And, young lady, don't you go raising your voice," her mother said. "And don't you think this pains me? Why can't you children think of anyone else for a change? And it's only for a little while that he's leaving. Don't you think we should be grateful that Mr. Noah Bell is alive?"

Olive walked out of the room and came back with something in one hand. Covering Mr. Bell's fresh clothes, she carefully rubbed flour into his damp hair, eyebrows, and beard. The gray hair made a big difference. No one could recognize him now.

"Dinah, will you take care of your mother?" he asked.

She wiped tears off her cheeks. Take care of her mother? He hadn't asked how they had managed without him; why they were living in a cellar; how they had paid the rent; or how they had bought food.

Dinah sighed. Her father had never known about their children's humbug. All her father cared about was his work for justice. She forgave him for that. She nodded yes: she would take care of her mother.

The two men lifted Papa, and he leaned on them; he was moving stiffly and tottering along the floor. After Dinah and her mother hugged him, he held out his arms to the little Ruttenberg girls. Finally he patted Olive's shoulder and shook Ben's hand.

Raising his stiff hand, he said, "The Eight-Hour Day,

like the sun on a rainy afternoon, can be covered by clouds, but it will shine again." He chuckled. "All the mighty oak trees started as little nuts that held their ground."

The driver of the carriage outside jingled his bells.

"Wait," Dinah called. She dug in her pocket and handed her papa his rosary with the Coptic cross. He smiled and lifted it to his lips. After kissing the cross, he tucked the rosary in a pocket.

Dinah felt relieved when Ben jumped in the carriage. Now she knew her father would board that train safely. When she heard the carriage roll away, she glanced toward her mother.

Mrs. Mary Bell sat on the bed crying and rubbing her nub. Dinah ran to her, and they hugged. She kissed her mother on the cheek, then turned to her new little sisters. They looked frightened, but grinned when Dinah beckoned. One by one they came over for a hug, then all five embraced.

Tonight I better start teaching them English, Dinah thought. Tomorrow was Thursday, the day she, Ben, and Olive would begin to exchange work for food for the family.

They were poor in one sense, but her father's rescue had proved that they were rich in another. What more could you ask of friends and neighbors than to risk their lives for yours?

And, as her father said, in time that Eight-Hour Day would arrive, and it would be beautiful.

AUTHOR'S NOTE

To understand Chicago's Haymarket tragedy, we must understand the hunger and hopes of working people in May 1886. After the Great Chicago Fire of 1871 people in Europe and America donated millions of dollars to a Chicago Relief and Aid Society. The third of the population who had been burned out of homes and small businesses received little or none of that money. Instead, wealthy businessmen used the money for their rebuilding, and the middle class and poor grew more impoverished.

At the same time, Chicago was flooded with immigrants looking for a better life. In the 1880s Chicago went from a population of half a million to a population of over a million. And in the year before the Haymarket tragedy alone, 125,000 immigrants arrived. They were mostly German, Irish, Bohemian, Polish, Scandinavian, and Czech.

Companies in Chicago and across America used workers like machines. Laboring people worked in factories, mills, and coal mines for ten to fifteen hours a day—sixty to ninety hours a week. By the age of twelve, children had joined their parents in working. They no longer attended schools. Some businessmen felt education was bad for working-class children; it "spoiled" them for labor.

African-Americans, former slaves freed in the Civil War, also sought jobs in Chicago. Therefore, with thousands of immigrants and blacks begging for jobs, owners could lock out workers who complained and hire new workers.

Living conditions were miserable. Chicago's tenement housing was sometimes unheated in winter and had no indoor toilets or water; several families were often crowded into a single roach- and rat-infested room.

Whole families starved; homeless people slept in hallways of tenements and in tunnels under the Chicago River. Those with jobs often worked at near-starvation wages. However, wealthy people who owned businesses—such as lumberyards, sawmills, farm-machinery factories, meatpacking plants, shoemaking shops, and sewing mills—became millionaires.

Furthermore, the poor worked long hours with no provision for health care, injuries, or old age. Many machines were dangerous. Workers were fined for broken parts, tardiness, and factory improvements. Workers had to take an ironclad oath not to join unions, and those fired for being in unions, or on strikes, were blacklisted so that they couldn't be rehired anywhere.

Wealthy owners used Pinkerton's National Detective Agency to control worker discontent and to infiltrate unions as spies.

Finally workers decided a shorter workday would share jobs and provide more-humane and safer working conditions.

In 1884 the Federation of Organized Trades and Labor Unions of the United States and Canada set May 1, 1886, as the day to march and strike for the Eight-Hour Day. In Chicago eighty thousand marched down

Michigan Avenue that Saturday. Jubilant as they marched, they felt they were sending a message that they wanted to share their jobs with those out of work.

Sunday, May 2, was quiet except for small parades and celebrations. Monday, May 3, striking lumber shovers met on Black Road near the McCormick Reaper Factory. When bells rang and workers left McCormick's, metalworkers who had been locked out from McCormick's strolled over to jeer and throw stones at the newly hired workers. Police arrived and began shooting and clubbing the locked-out workers, killing two and injuring many.

To protest that police brutality, workers planned a meeting in Haymarket Square for the evening of Tuesday, May 4. Since the crowd was small, the first speaker climbed on a wagon by Crane's Alley on Desplaines Street, about fifty feet from Haymarket Square.

As the last of three speakers was finishing, a cold drizzle began, and the crowd of about twenty-five hundred dwindled to two hundred. The mayor, who had attended earlier, told the police captain to dismiss his policemen because the meeting was peaceful.

However, shortly after the mayor left, police led by Captain John Bonfield marched onto the crowd. At that point a dynamite bomb was thrown. Again the police began shooting and clubbing people. Many workers were killed or injured. One policeman soon bled to death, and other officers died later.

First, eleven, then eight activists—the Haymarket Eight—were blamed for the death of the first policeman. They were considered conspirators of the bomb thrower; however, to this day no one is sure who threw the bomb.

Four men were hanged: August Spies; Albert Parsons, who left, then returned to stand trial with his friends; Adolph Fischer; and George Engel. One man, Louis Lingg, died a suspicious death in his jail cell. Three— Oscar Neebe, Samuel Fielden, and Michael Schwab— were jailed and later pardoned.

Illinois governor John Peter Altgeld pardoned them because he realized that the trial was unfair, that the rulings of the court were illegal, and that their sentences were unjust. Contrary to freedom of speech, the men were sentenced for what they had said, rather than for what they had done.

Nevertheless, the Haymarket tragedy was an excuse for a crackdown on trade unions across the United States. Leaders were arrested and charged with rioting and conspiracy in Pittsburgh, Milwaukee, and New York.

Mrs. Lucy Parsons led an international protest movement. Unions in France, Italy, Spain, Russia, Holland, and England worked in vain to save the condemned leaders. However, businessmen felt there would be less discontent after the men were hanged. Indeed, the Haymarket tragedy did slow labor's momentum and the Eight-Hour Day Movement in America.

Three years later police captains Bonfield and Schaak were arrested for various kinds of corruption.

Almost fifty years later, in 1935, a national ruling established an eight-hour day under President Franklin Delano Roosevelt's Fair Labor Standards Act.

My characters Dinah, Olive, Ben, and their families are fictional; but other people and details are true to the best of my research. And my fictional characters are examples of people who might have lived at that time.

Labor unions still work toward more jobs, better working conditions, decent wages, less overtime, better low-income housing, and benefits such as health insurance and retirement.

Today's labor struggle needs young people to know the story of labor, to understand the problems of working people, and to work for social justice.

BIBLIOGRAPHY

Adelman, William J. *Haymarket Revisited*. Chicago: Illinois Labor History Society, 1976.

Avrich, Paul. *The Haymarket Tragedy*. Princeton, New Jersey: Princeton University Press, 1984.

Boyer, Richard, and Herbert Morais. *Labor's Untold Story*. Pittsburgh: United Electrical, Radio and Machine Workers of America, 1955.

David, Henry. *The History of the Haymarket Affair*. New York: Farrar & Rinehart, 1936.

Kebabian, John S., et. al. *The Haymarket Affair and the Trial of the Chicago Anarchists, 1886*. New York: H. P. Kraus, 1970.

Parsons, Lucy E. *Life of Albert Parsons with a Brief History of the Labor Movement in America*. Chicago: Mrs. Albert Parsons, Publisher and Proprietor, 1889.

Roediger, Dave, and Franklin Rosemont, eds. *Haymarket Scrapbook*. Chicago: Charles H. Kerr Publishing Company, 1986.

Smith, Carl. *Urban Disorder and the Shape of Belief: The Great Chicago Fire, the Haymarket Bomb, and the Model Town of Pullman*. Chicago: University of Chicago Press, 1995.

Trager, James. *The People's Chronology*. New York: Henry Holt, 1992.